# Quantrill's Legacy

At the end of the Civil War there followed the greatest move westward that the American continent had ever known. These were men so different from one another, following ideals so utterly opposed that they only had one thing in common – they fought and died by the law of the gun and could spit in the face of death and laugh.

When Lee Devrin came back from the war, he found his house burnt, his family killed by Quantrill's Raiders, and the parasitical carpetbaggers from the north moving in to claim everything from an impoverished state. It was this strange alchemy of fate that turned Devrin from an optimistic youth to an embittered man. Lee took to the gun trail which led from one end of Missouri to the other – a trail with only death waiting at the end of it. He rode with a trace of a tight smile on his dust-caked face, eyes deep blue and much too old and world weary for a young man, his hand never far removed from the smooth butt of the gun at his waist.

# Quantrill's Legacy

Robert L. Greene

A Black Horse Western

ROBERT HALE · LONDON

© 1966, 2003 John Glasby
First hardcover edition 2003
Originally published in paperback as
*Guntrail* by Tex Bradley

ISBN 0 7090 7244 9

Robert Hale Limited
Clerkenwell House
Clerkenwell Green
London EC1R 0HT

Typeset by
Derek Doyle & Associates, Liverpool.
Printed and bound in Great Britain by
Antony Rowe Limited, Wiltshire

# WHO RIDES WITH QUANTRILL

At times during the early morning, before the full heat of high noon made walking and riding intolerable, small groups of men, sometimes with covered wagons, moved into the tiny Mexican town of San Randido. They moved only one way along the street, gathering in the tiny square, the men swinging down from the saddles and tailboards and moving off into the various cantinas along the narrow, cobbled streets.

Hague Bassard had stood at the window of the small villa overlooking the square most of the morning and watched the men move in. He saw the dust-caked men walking their horses, the brims of their hats pulled low over their dark-tanned faces, men who swayed in the wagons, the reins grasped loosely in their hands. There were a few other riders moving into the town; Saturday morning brought a great many kinds of men in from the surrounding area. Prospectors from the hills, a few flat-bed wagons with a man and woman on the tongue, possibly a handful of kids in the back. But he scarcely gave these people a second glance.

A knock on the door made him turn. Going across the room, he opened the door, stepped to one side to allow the man who stood there to enter.

'You have any trouble on the way here, Ben?'

'No. Everything went just as we figured.' Ben Gifford was tall, lean and hard, with a tight mouth under a thin, black moustache and an air of jaunty confidence. His tone was deprecating as he went on: 'The war seems to be going our way at the moment. Plenty of loot to be had along the southern border. We still need guns and ammunition though. This won't be the last load we run in for Quantrill.'

'Just so long as he keeps paying I've got no quarrel with that.' Bassard motioned the other to a chair, went over to the small cupboard in the corner and took out a bottle and two glasses, bringing them over to the window. He poured the drinks, then sat down himself, raising his glass. 'Here's to Quantrill and our business deal with him,' he said, a faint mocking overtone to his voice.

'I'll sure drink to that.' Gifford swallowed his drink noisily, grimaced a little as the raw liquor went down. 'I needed that,' he said harshly. 'It's been hard on the trail this time. Most of the waterholes along the border are dried up. We'll need to take a few more barrels back with us. Can you arrange that?'

'I reckon so. I'll be riding back with you this time.'

This was certainly news to Gifford, but he gave no outward sign of surprise. 'You got more of that whiskey?' he asked. 'Takes more'n one glass to wash the trail dust out of a man's throat.'

'Help yourself.' Bassard nodded towards the bottle on the table. He got to his feet and walked back to his place at the window, staring down into the street. The shadows were shortening rapidly now as the blazing disc of the sun lifted to its zenith. White dust lay almost an inch deep in the centre of the street; and already the heat head was reaching its piled-up intensity, pressing down on every-thing in a shimmering, half-seen blanket of superheated air which made the outlines of the adobe buildings shiver as though he were viewing them through a layer of water.

Most of the wagons had now arrived. He let his glance run along them where they stood in a line around the far perimeter of the square. A dozen of them. Another three to come in. Then they would be ready to begin loading them up with guns and ammunition.

'Where are Buck and the others?'

Gifford paused with the glass half raised to his lips. 'They took the Guacharaha trail across the Badlands. Buck figured it would be a shorter trail and there was talk of water along the route. Guess he found it longer than he figured.'

'Just so long as they get here within the next day or so. Quantrill doesn't like anything to go wrong or to be kept waiting for supplies.'

'You don't have to remind me of that,' nodded the other in affirmation. 'That man is a real terror. Sometimes I reckon he's fighting both sides in this war. They both sure would like to get their hands on him.'

'I know. That's why he has to get his arms from this side of the border.' Bassard drained the glass in his hand, set it down on the dusty window ledge. Sooner or later, he reflected, with a faint tinge of apprehension in his mind, Quantrill was going to get himself caught. He was playing a dangerous game, raiding the towns and trails of the southern states. With detachments of both armies on the look out for him, it was only a matter of time before he made the one mistake which would be his last. The war too, would soon be over, one way or the other, and when that happened, the law, in the shape of the Army or some other form, would be free to concentrate on capturing him and those who rode with him. He rubbed his chin thoughtfully. Maybe it would not be a bad thing as far as he personally was concerned, to look for a judicious moment to pull out of this business. The longer he stayed in it, did the dirty work for Quantrill, the more dangerous it would be.

But there would still be the need for caution. These men who had brought in the wagons, men such as Gifford here; it was impossible to tell who could be trusted and who might inform Quantrill of his intentions. Far better to keep such thoughts to himself for the time being.

'You look like you've got something on your mind, Hague,' said Gifford after a while.

'Why do you say that?'

Gifford shrugged. 'Just the impression I got watching you. You're standing at that window like a caged animal.'

'Just wondering how long this can go on for us, that's all.'

Gifford uttered a harsh laugh. 'It'll go on as long as the war goes on, Hague; make no mistake about that. When you get two sides at each other's throats as they are right now, they don't have much time to take care of a third party.'

'And once the war is over?' Bassard turned and gave the other a sharp glance. 'It won't go on for ever and no matter which side wins eventually, they'll do their best to stamp us out.'

Gifford's grin remained, but it was fixed and stretched taut now. 'The war ain't over yet and as soon as there are any signs of it ending, we can be over the border in a little town like this with nothing to worry about for the rest of our lives.' He hesitated, then went on, his tone a little sharper than before, edged with suspicion. 'You're not going soft on us are you, Hague?'

Bassard gave a quick shake of his head. 'Nothing like that.' He moved over to the door. 'Let's go have a talk with the others.'

The four men in the small cantina looked up sharply as the doors swung wide and Bassard and Gifford walked in, blinking in the gloom of the interior. Bassard held up two fingers, catching the Mexican's eye, then walked over to the table, studying the men already seated there. Three of them, he knew well; the fourth, a tall, hard-eyed man was a stranger to him. Bassard looked coldly at him. The silence dragged and then Claythorne, face still smeared with yellow trail dust said:

'This is Clem Monaghan, Hague.'

Bassard gave the other a brief nod of acknowledgement. 'You're sure he's all right?'

Shankland, seated on the far side of the table muttered: 'Quantrill asked us to bring him along on this trip.'

'Quantrill?'

'That's right, Bassard,' said Monaghan softly. His tone sounded just a shade too confident for Bassard's liking. 'Maybe he's not too sure that everything is all right at this end. I understand he wants you to ride back with us on this occasion.'

Bassard felt a sharp rise of anger, controlled it with an effort, noticing the faint sneer on the other's features.

Picking up his drink, he drank it slowly, watching the other closely over the rim of his glass. Inwardly, he felt troubled, tried not to show it. It was instantly obvious that Monaghan had been sent there to spy on him, keep him under close surveillance.

'I've never failed to deliver the goods to Quantrill yet,' he said coldly, setting down his glass. 'I reckon that the rest of these men can vouch for that.'

9

Monaghan shrugged. 'It's of little interest to me. I just do as Quantrill says.' He studied Bassard over a moment of thoughtful silence, then leaned back in his chair. 'When do you reckon on riding out again?'

'Two, maybe three, days. It'll take that long to load up with arms and supplies. Most of the way is across desert and we can't afford to take too little water for the journey. We'll be eating hard tack and drinking cold water before we get back.'

'That doesn't worry me any.' Monaghan finished the drink in his glass, set it down and took out a long, thin cheroot, lit it and blew smoke nonchalantly into the air. There was no expression on his face. 'It's better than fighting in the wilderness. Only trouble we're likely to have will be from a detachment of the Army if we're unlucky enough to run into them on the way back. You figure they might be on the look out for us?'

'That's more'n likely,' Bassard conceded. 'They've taken to watching the trails leading up from the border since Quantrill's last raids. Reckon they have to try to do something about it even though there is a war going on.' He gave the other a closer scrutiny. 'You worried about running into trouble like that, Monaghan?'

'No,' said the other flatly. Bassard noticed that the smooth, measured tone had been replaced by a harsh and authoritative inflection – the tone of a man who was accustomed to being obeyed if he ever gave an order. Keeping his glance fixed on the other as Monaghan puffed at the cheroot, he decided that he might have to revise his first impression of him. Monaghan had struck him as being something of the flashy type, more of a dude than a man accustomed to a gunfight. But now, he figured, there was steel somewhere in the other and it might be unwise to sell him short, particularly if Monaghan had been sent through to Mexico to see that nothing went wrong with the shipments of arms to Quantrill, or that any of the men had ideas of pulling out in case things got tough.

Later that evening, back in his room at the hotel, Bassard stood near the window, looking out at the deepening purple of the twilight, pondering on the real reason why Monaghan was there in San Randido. For a moment, the idea came to him to pull out, to get away from this place and move further into Mexico. It was possible that nobody would bother to come after him and if he rode out that night, it would give him several hours start before anyone moved out to trail him. He lifted his gaze and stared out at the country which lay beyond the town. This raw, naked, red sandstone country was even more open than many parts of Texas and just as barren and uninviting. Wide, sandy stretches of ground rimmed around with the flat-topped mesas, some times with their upper reaches hidden by the clouds and at others, gleaming with a strange copper light in the full glare of the sun.

A chilly gust of air swept in through the half-open window and he pulled up the collar of his shirt, then closed the window, moved back into the room. A second later, he paused, edged forward slowly and peered cautiously out. The dark silhouette, just visible near the low-roofed adobe had moved a little, gave away its presence there by the faintly pulsing orange glow of a cigarette or a slender cheroot. He pressed himself tightly against the wall so as not to show himself and tried to make out the identity of the man who seemed to be more than usually interested in the window of his room. He felt reasonably certain that it was Monaghan down there, keeping a close watch on him and once again, that feeling of anger swept through him. Lowering his hand, he rested his fingers on the butt of the Colt at his waist, then withdrew them slowly. That was not the way to go about this, he reflected. Better to play along with the other until he discovered for himself what lay behind this. He had no wish to fall foul of Quantrill at the moment.

However dangerous Monaghan might be, he was nothing compared with Quantrill. That man was a real devil. But there was certainly something faintly off-centre about Monaghan. He knew now though that it would not be smart to try to get out of San Randido and head deeper into Mexico.

A few moments later, the man moved away from the adobe. Even then it was impossible for Bassard to be sure who the other was. Certainly he was the same build as Monaghan but beyond that he could not be sure. He saw the man drop his smoke on to the ground, rub it out under his heel, throw one last look up at the window and then move off into the long, square shadows of the surrounding buildings.

Three days later, they hit north, leaving San Randido shortly before dawn and riding all day and most of the following night. The country through which they passed was wild and broken, a tangled stretch of chaparral and catsclaw, growing in dense profusion on banks of low rock and thin topsoil.

Shortly before dawn, Bassard called a halt. Most of the men were drowsing in their saddles, the high collars of their mackinaw jackets pulled up around their necks in a vain effort to keep off the bitterly cold wind that bit through them.

Monaghan rode up, skirting the line of wagons. There was a faintly sardonic expression on his leanly handsome features. 'You figure this is a good place to make camp, Bassard?' His gaze flickered about him, eyeing the trail where it widened out before rushing closely together again as the broad shoulders of the buttes pressed down tightly against it, running it into a canyon.

12

'Best spot for fifty miles or more,' Bassard grunted non-committally. 'We can post a couple of men up on top of the buttes and they'll be able to scan the trail in both directions.'

Monaghan seemed satisfied, shrugged and turned away, walking his mount to the nearest wagon where he bent and took a long drink from the water barrel hitched against the side.

Curl leaf was found and a quick, hot fire made that was virtually smokeless. Bassard sat on the edge of the fireglow, eating the bacon and beans, washing them down with the hot black coffee. He had a great deal to think about and although a little of it was in the past, nearly all of it was to do with the future. He felt the muscles draw tight under his ribs as he looked forward to the inevitable meeting with Quantrill. There had to be some important reason why the other wanted him on this trip, why he had sent Monaghan to watch his every move. Could it be that Quantrill suspected him? Did he guess at the thoughts that were in his mind? No, that was quite impossible. He tried to shrug the idea away but with very little success. Doubt attacked him from many angles. What did Quantrill have in store for him? He knew only too well just how ruthless the other could be. There were so many complex emotions driving the other on that no man could ever really understand him. But one thing he did insist on, one thing he believed he had every right to expect, was undying loyalty from the men who rode with him.

Where was an answer as far as he was concerned? He shifted himself a little further back from the red glow of the fire as Gifford tossed more twigs on to it, sending the red sparks spiralling upward through the tangled mass of piney stuff above them. Across the fire he saw that Monaghan was watching him again as he had been all the way out from San Randido. He let his own glance slide away from the other's. Just what sort of ideas were running through that man's mind at that moment? he wondered briefly.

Two resolves became definite in his mind. Once they got to where Quantrill was hiding out, he would tell the other all that he had decided, put it to him on the line. There was no way of telling how the other would take the news, that was a risk he would have to take himself. The other resolve was that no matter what happened, he did not intend to ride with Quantrill again on one of the other's raids on unarmed, or poorly armed, people whose only crime was that they had somehow incurred Quantrill's displeasure. Sometimes, in the past, Bassard felt certain that there had not even been this flimsy excuse. Quantrill had burned their farms to the ground, killed innocent men and women just because of some inner, driving force of evil in him . . . .

Morning, and the wagon train moved north, through the narrow canyon and out into more open, dusty country. Riding was hard. monotonous and mean; the yellow-white dust working its way between their clothing and skin, itching and abrading, filled their boots and forced its way into their mouths, eyes and nostrils. All around them there was a silence so deep and still that it pressed against them with a tangible effect that could be felt as well as sensed.

Stretching out before them, as far as the eye could see, was desert. It reached to the far horizons, it lay in great, sun-shimmering waves all about them, throwing back the heat and the glare in sickening, dizzying pulses that brought the sweat boiling from their bodies, brought it rolling down their foreheads and backs where it mingled with the dust until the agony was scarcely bearable. The men driving the wagons had it the worst. They had no chance to get out of the dust kicked up by the others.

They checked their mounts on a rise of ground that

looked out over the broad trail still leading them north and west. Tired men who had ridden far and fast. Bassard lifted a hand, felt himself swaying in the saddle from weariness. The wagons formed their inevitable circle and the riders moved their horses towards the small waterhole a quarter of a mile away, watering their mounts before leading them back to camp.

Bassard studied the sky, watching the cloud formations as the sun went down, towering dark cumulus moving high over the western horizon, mingling greyly with the reds and golds.

'Chances are we'll sleep wet tonight,' he observed.

Monaghan grinned. 'I reckon we're all used to that,' he opined. 'At least we'll have plenty of water for the rest of the trail if it does rain.'

The storm broke just after the rich colours in the west faded. A dark grey cloud swept in fast from the horizon, blotting out the first sky sentinels. The last pale yellow streaks of sunset faded abruptly and a chill wind came in just ahead of the storm. The horses were ground reined close to the wagons and the men huddled down near the fire, their collars turned up high against the coming fury of the storm. There was the rumble of thunder, still in the distance, but heading closer. Lightning forked the heavens to the west of them, lacing the darkening sky with a network of brilliant, arcing streaks of fire. The thunder rumbled close on their heels and a curtain of rain struck at the men as they crouched near the wagons. Wind built up and shrieked at the canvas, whipping it around the metal uprights. Within seconds, everyone at the fire was drenched to the skin as the torrent of raindrops fell, hissing, into the flames.

There was no protecting ledge or ridge for miles where they might find any shelter. Apart from the low rise on which they were now camped, the ground was as flat as a table in every direction. Shivering, Bassard pulled out his blankets, drew them beneath one of the wagons and worked his way into them, listening to the dismal rattle of the rain as it dropped from the sides of the wagon, streaming on to the sandy ground which sucked it up avidly until it could hold no more, so that it lay in widening puddles all about the camp.

Daybreak found them digging the wagons out of the sodden ruts into which their weight had thrust them. Straining and cursing, the men added their strength to that of the horses to push them free and even when they were rolling once again, the wheels continued to bog down in the sodden, muddy earth. Progress was slower than they had anticipated. The men swayed in their saddles, bodies caked with sand, their faces yellow masks through which only their eyes showed, dark and haunted. Fifteen miles a day, sometimes twenty or twenty-five, long miles that were ridden mostly in silence, each man engrossed in his own thoughts, tired, smarting eyes that looked out over the endless plains and lifting buttes. Trail-weary riders dozed in their saddles as they put another and yet another mile behind them. Until on the fifteenth day they rode into wide reaches of grass, peppered with stands of thick brush, and criss-crossed by tiny, swift-running streams. They nooned at a small creek under a high clump of tall cedars.

By the time the sun had left its zenith and was drawing slowly down the sky towards the western horizon, they were on the move again, on the last stretch of the journey. Beyond the creek, the brush grew thicker, interspersed with chaparral and it was not until late in the afternoon that they finally rode clear of it, moving out on to a well-used trail which they followed into the wild, rocky country that loomed up on the near horizon.

Another half hour brought them to the small settlement hidden away among the rocks. It was really no more than a perceptible widening of the trail, with a tumbledown store and a few wooden buildings that leaned lopsidedly on either side of the trail. Several horses were hitched outside one of the buildings and a group of men loafed near the door, pitching horseshoes around a short wooden stake in the ground.

The men were laughing hoarsely as the wagon train rounded the bend in the trail, the harsh sound of their voices blending with the sharp ring of the metal as the shoes whanged against each other near the pin. Bassard recognised several of the men, guessed that Quantrill would be somewhere close by, possibly inside the building, planning another raid.

Bassard edged his mount forward, waved the wagons to move into single file along the trail. Reining up in front of the solitary two-storey building, he slid wearily from the saddle, eased a cramped leg, then went inside, letting the doors swing shut behind him on creaking hinges. He felt shaky all over, but tried not to show it. Slapping the dust from his jacket, he glanced about him. Quantrill was seated at one of the round wooden tables near the bar, with three of his lieutenants with him.

He waited a moment before going over to the others. Quantrill, sensing a fraction of his reaction, looked up sharply.

'You should have arrived two days ago,' he said harshly. 'What happened?'

'We ran into a storm,' Bassard said. He stood behind Carraway, directly opposite Quantrill.

'I'm in,' Quantrill said, glancing down at the cards he held in his hand. He took five of the chips off the top of the stack in front of him and tossed them negligently into the middle of the table.

The man on his left threw down his cards, said in a disgusted tone. 'I fold. No luck at all today.'

Quantrill uttered a harsh laugh, then as though remembering that Bassard was still standing there, said: 'You ran into a storm then?'

'That's right. Maybe you ain't seen that desert after it really rains. The wagons were all heavy loaded like you asked and pushing 'em through that mud was as much as we could manage.'

Quantrill gave a brief nod. 'You want to sit in, Bassard?' His tone was deceptively mild, too quiet.

The other hesitated, then pulled out a chair and sat down, waited until that hand was finished with Quantrill raking in the pot, then sat forward in his chair, taking the pile of chips that Carraway pushed towards him.

Quantrill dealt out the hand and Bassard picked up his five cards, staring at them with only half of his attention. He knew that sooner or later, Quantrill was going to get to the point of why he had asked him to ride north with the train, but that nothing in the world would hurry the other. He had the unshakable feeling that Quantrill was using this poker game to feel him out, to try to judge him, get at what might lie behind his thoughts. Maybe, he reflected, Quantrill wasn't quite as sure of himself now that they had met face to face as he had felt before. The thought gave his jaded spirits a lift and he forced himself to concentrate on the game.

There were two queens in his hand and he placed his chips in the pot. All of them stayed in for that round and glancing at the three cards dealt him, he found another lady, the nine and the ace of spades.

'Carraway?' said Quantrill.

'I reckon I'll play these,' murmured the other.

Bassard eyed Carraway closely, decided that the other was bluffing. The man just didn't have a poker face.

Quantrill must have reached that conclusion too for he merely gave a tight little smile and sat back in his chair, picking up the three cards one at a time and fitting them very carefully into his hand. He pushed three chips away from him, sliding them across the polished wood with the tips of his well-manicured fingers.

'You know why I asked you to come here on this trip, Bassard?'

For a second, the other paused, hand outstretched, clutching his chips. Then he shrugged, placed them on top of the pile in the centre of the table and said nonchalantly: 'I guessed it had to be something pretty important, though I can't guess what it is. I figured I was doing a good job for you in Mexico.'

'So you were,' nodded the other. His keen-eyed gaze flicked to Bassard's face. 'But it occurred to me that you might feel out of it down there across the border. You've been in San Randido for almost a year now. Monaghan will be taking your place. He'll ride back with the next train. I want you here with me.'

'Sure, if that's the way you want it.'

'It is.' A faintly sardonic smile played around Quantrill's lips for a moment. 'Now that we have fresh guns and ammunition, it's time we rode out once more. You'll be riding with us.'

Suddenly it was clear to Bassard that he should have known it before, but this brought it out into the open with no words wasted. Quantrill did not trust him, considered him to be of little, if no, importance. Sitting there, he felt a sharp sense of self-consciousness and he was suddenly angry at knowing this. He felt a flush come to his face and a sharp retort rose to his lips, was bitten down quickly before anything could be uttered.

Sardonically, Quantrill said: 'You were on the point of saying something?'

Bassard swallowed thickly. He shook his head. 'Nothing of any importance,' he muttered tautly.

'I thought so,' Quantrill's lips parted. 'We seem to be the only two left in the game, Bassard. What you going to do?'

Fumbling a little with his chips, conscious of the stares of the other men on him, Bassard picked up five of them and tossed them into the middle. 'I'm in.' His fingers tightened convulsively on his cards.

Quantrill eyed him closely for a moment, evidently undecided whether or not he was bluffing, then said: 'I'll see you, Bassard.'

'Three ladies.' Bassard spread his cards face up on the table. A gust of expression passed over the other's face, then he smiled again, forcing it this time. 'Beats me,' he said softly, exposing two pairs. 'That's enough for me right now. We've got to get the rest of the men a place to sleep and something to eat. The unloading of the wagons can wait until tomorrow.'

Carraway looked at him in surprise, eyes wide, then they closed down to a slight squint. He pushed back his chair, got to his feet, moving towards the doors. The rest of the men did likewise and Bassard took this as a dismissal, heaved himself wearily to his feet and moved away.

'Bassard!' Quantrill swung round in his chair, legs thrust out straight in front of him. He waited, sucking his teeth, making sure that the other would stay: 'Bassard . . . you've carried out my orders without question in the past. That's why I want you to ride with us tomorrow night. You've had it easy down there in Mexico with no trouble, you sleep well at nights and get plenty of good food to eat, wine to drink whenever you want it. I figure it would be wise to make sure that this kind of life hasn't softened you at all.'

Bassard pressed his lips tightly together for a moment, searching for some answer to what was almost an accusation. 'I don't know why you should think that,' he said finally, lamely.

'Just an idea I got,' said the other, his tone almost pleasant. 'I don't like my men to be out of touch with the harsh realities of this war for too long. They tend to forget what we're doing, and the way we do things. I'll admit that this isn't a regular Army unit, but we do have to have a chain of command and orders which are obeyed without question. Otherwise we would break up within weeks.'

We're nothing more than a bunch of mercenaries, Bassard thought inwardly; and wondered why this was the first time he had realised that. Now he saw them all for what they really were. A ragged army of killers, rapists, looters; all joined together by the domination of this one man.

'So where do I come in?' he asked, moistening his lips with the tip of his tongue.

Quantrill smiled. 'Now that's more like it.' He waved to the man behind the bar. 'There's a bunch of ranches about thirty miles north of here who've been giving us trouble lately. I reckon it's time they were taught a lesson.'

'You think they'll fight?'

'Could be. But since when have you been scared of that? Besides, most of the men who can handle a gun are away at the front. We won't run into much trouble. A handful of women, old men. By the time we're through with them, they won't be giving anybody any more trouble.' His smile became suddenly cold and vicious.

'I see.' Bassard could think of nothing more to say in the circumstances. He knew that Quantrill was waiting, watching him, to see if he intended to back out.

'You got nothing else to say?' queried Quantrill. He gulped down the whiskey that was placed in front of him.

From outside came the harsh shouts of the men still toss-ing horseshoes.

Bassard seemed to hear everything with a curiously magnified sense, as if his hearing had suddenly become very acute. He was vaguely aware of the thud of his own blood through his veins and his heart thumping against his ribs. He muttered: 'Don't see that there's anything more to say.'

Quantrill grinned. 'That's what I like in a man. The ability to accept the inevitable with a good grace. It saves a lot of time and trouble.'

The ranch house was a dark square, silhouetted against the pale flood of white moonlight that laid an eerie glow over the scene. The bunch of men had reined their horses on the low, wooded rise that looked down over the ranch. Quantrill, a little in front of the other suddenly turned in his saddle, motioned to Bassard to ride up to him.

Pointing, he said tightly: 'I had a couple of my men scout out this place a few days ago. Only the women and an old man. Nothing to worry us. We'll take them from all sides, fire the barn and then the house.'

'You know these folks?'

'Name's Devrin,' said Quantrill. 'Them and their neigh-bours have been talking of getting together a Vigilante Organisation and riding us out of the territory so I figure we should pay them a visit and get in our blow first. If we was to leave them alone, they might get enough men together to be a nuisance to us.'

'A woman and an old man can't be too much of a danger to us.' Bassard said and knew the moment he uttered the words that it was the wrong thing to say.

At once, Quantrill's expression changed, became hard and vicious. 'Just as I had it figured, Bassard. You're getting soft. Too much easy living south of the border.

Well this is one time that you fight. I don't want any of these folk left alive by morning, not one stone standing on another. Maybe when the others in the territory see how we handle them, they'll think twice about deciding to go up against me.'

Anger battled for a moment through the faint chill of fear which had settled on Bassard's mind. Then he saw the other's hand drop towards the gun at his waist, thought better of it, and pulled around the head of his horse. He rode through the knee-high grass to join the rest of the men.

'Don't try to argue things out with him, Bassard,' said Carraway softly. 'You won't get anywhere and you may even stop a bullet. He don't take too kindly to anything like that.'

Bassard gave a quick nod, said nothing. The other had evidently meant this as a piece of friendly advice, but he could still not rid his mind of the twisting sense of revulsion at the thought of what they had come here to do. He guessed that the folk here were virtually defenceless, that they could not hope to stand up to the combined gunfire which could be thrown at them from all sides. This would be nothing short of sheer, cold-blooded murder. He felt sick to the bottom of his stomach, but knew that there was no way out for him. It would have been far better as far as he was concerned if he had taken that slim chance of getting out of San Randido during that night when he had spotted Monaghan watching his window in the small hotel. By now, he could have been several hundred miles away, out of reach of Quantrill and these killers.

He sighed audibly. All of that was in the past now. A man could never go back and cover the same part of the trail twice. He had made a mistake that night and it was irrevocable, done, and there was now no way out for him.

Glancing out of the corner of his eye at Quantrill,

where the other sat tall and straight in the saddle, he saw that the man's eyes had that peculiar glazed look which he had seen on several occasions in the past. The other's senses were sealed off. He had the look of a man who had rehearsed this thing a hundred times and would not be cheated of its fulfilment now no matter what happened. A man who had vowed to himself; vowed to kill. To kill and destroy without thought or mercy; without weakness. For him there would be no mollycoddling or understanding or forgiveness. Quantrill did not understand these qualities in a man, considered them to be merely a sign of weakness, something which could never be tolerated.

Hard-faced and hard-eyed, he signalled his men to move forward. Bassard tightened, felt his knees tremble a little, but he did not move. A rifle shot rang out and Bassard jerked upright in the saddle, strained his vision to peer into the clinging darkness. For a second, he thought that one of the advancing men had fired the shot. Then he saw that it had come from one of the windows of the small ranch house. The faint puff of smoke was just visible, hovering in the still air and at the very edge of his vision, he saw one of the men wavering in the saddle, clinging with a frightened frenzy to the saddlehorn for support. He uttered a low, moaning whimper, then lost his grip and pitched sideways, hitting the ground with a hard thump.

'Give them a volley,' roared Quantrill. He drew his gun and loosed off several shots at the building. Bullets crashed into the walls and shattered the windows as the men in the party moved around to take it from all sides. Hauling his horse back among the trees, Bassard stared down at the scene in front of him. He had a curiously creepy feeling about it all and a small moment of panic made his fingers clench convulsively on the reins, knuckles standing out white under the skin. He clenched his teeth together so tightly in his mouth that pain lanced through the muscles of his jaw.

The firing swung around as more shots came from the smashed windows. It seemed no longer to be pouring against the side facing him but smashing into the back of the house towards which most of the party had moved. The intensity of that smashing volley was terrible. The shattering sound seemed to vibrate through his skull, shaking his brain like the kernel inside a walnut. The utter savage destruction shook him to the very roots of his soul. He heard the solid jar of lead as it flailed through the flimsy wooden walls, took away the last splinters of glass in the windows. He heard the harsh yells of the men as they swung from their saddles and crawled closer to the house, crouching down behind the water troughs and near the wooden uprights of the small corral.

Sucking in a sharp breath he tried to shut his mind, his ears and eyes to everything. Every single muscle in him was drawn so tight that his whole body ached. The muscles of his legs were cramped, shot through and through with lances of agony and his mind seemed, for some strange reason, to be very sharp, magnifying everything. He could follow the shifting weight of the attack quite easily, tried to discern Quantrill, wondering if the other had noticed that he was taking no active part in the assault.

Three men, darkly-seen silhouettes, ran for the barn. There was a sudden splash of orange light as the grass-tarred torches were lit. The men vanished inside and Bassard lost sight of them for several moments. When they reappeared there was a flickering glow at their backs, highlighting them in the light of the flames. Dimly, above the rattle of gunfire, Bassard heard a faint yell from the house, caught the red stiletto of flame as a gun barked and saw one of the running shadows reel and fall. His two companions, bent, hauled him to his feet and pulled him along with them out of the line of fire, his boots dragging in the dust, spurs raking shallow channels in it.

Further off, other ranches that had been put to the torch, were beginning to blaze furiously in the night. Bassard felt a shudder go through him, swallowed thickly. This was not war as he knew it, he tried to tell himself. They were not fighting other armed men on equal terms. They were killing women and children, old men.

Only one gun was firing from the ranch house now and he caught intermittent glimpses of men moving in for the kill. He leaned forward in the saddle, shaking all over, not so much scared, as cowed, by the sheer destruction that was being executed before his eyes.

Half an hour later, the flames had a firm hold inside the house, the dry timber burning fiercely, sparks drifting across the courtyard. The roof too had caught fire and was blazing furiously.

Quantrill rode back up the rise, paused as he swung in the saddle to let his glance light on Bassard, his face a mask of bitter fury. 'Where the hell were you, Bassard?' he grunted. 'I didn't see you down there doing any fighting.'

'I—' Numbly, the other shook his head, knowing that there was nothing he could say.

'Better not say anything,' grated the other harshly. 'I'll deal with you myself when we get back. We still have discipline here whether you realise that or not.'

Spurring his mount, he rode back to join the rest of the men in the dusty courtyard, his features touched by the light of the fire so that they seemed to gleam with a diabolical glow. Bassard felt a shiver go through him. There was something of the devil in William Quantrill. He did not know it then, but this was the man who would, in a few months time, sack the town of Lawrence and put it to fire and sword.

# THE LONER

Hissing and steaming, the narrow gauge train pulled laboriously into the small town of Fenton, the black-grimed locomotive sending its plume of black smoke high into the still, sun-hazed air of the early afternoon. Stepping down from the rear coach, Lee Devrin alighted on the platform and stood for a moment looking about him, then he tipped back the broad-brimmed hat and wiped the back of his hand across his forehead. It had been hot and dusty inside the train during the long journey from Bent Springs; long, monotonous and mean. The single track led across some of the most desolate country in the State of Missouri, through the Badlands which lay to the west of the mountains. Here the elevation was such that he felt the welcome touch of coolness on his sun-burned face.

Bending, he picked up the small bag, gripping it tightly in his right hand, brushed some of the dust from the grey uniform and let his narrowed glance run over the rest of the passengers who had stepped down from the train. There were only three who had come the whole of the way from Calliston, the last stop along the line before Fenton. There were a couple of sharp-faced men, both with tell-tale bulges beneath their black frock-coats that spoke of hidden guns. He guessed they were gamblers, card-sharps, here to fleece the miners who panned for gold and silver in the hills. The third passenger was a tall, fair-haired woman. As she turned and looked back along the platform he had a fleeting glimpse of brows drawn level over clear grey eyes; the look of a woman who did not smile often, a woman of depth who seldom showed her emotions or feelings. Then she had turned away, passed through the small wicket gate at the far end, vanishing from his sight.

He walked slowly along the platform, passing the hissing engine, presented his ticket to the collector and went out into the wide, dusty street. Opposite the station house stood a hotel, with a saloon situated on either side of it and a livery stable a little further along the street. Devrin took in all of this in a single, sweeping glance, then let his gaze flick back towards the nearer of the two saloons. His first need was for a drink to wash the dust of the long, hot journey from his throat. Then to get himself a room for the night and arrange to buy a horse to take him on the last stage of his journey.

Pushing open the doors, he stepped inside, into the shadow and the coolness, moving up to the bar. A quick glance in the mirror behind the counter and he saw all that went on at his back. There were several men in the saloon for it was the full heat of the day. Most of the tables were occupied. Men played poker or faro, or sat in small groups, drinking and smoking.

The bartender regarded him across the counter, let his close scrutiny slide over Devrin's uniform, noticing the frayed edges and the tattered patches, every one of which told its own story.

Lee Devrin was home from the war, back from the terror, the bloodshed, the cannon roar and the singing bullet that brought death striking out of the silent blackness of the night and the tangled green of the thickets in the wilderness where the last great battle had been fought and the South had met defeat. The war had wrought a great change in him, had changed him from a boy into a man; had forced him to witness death close at hand, kneeling beside a dying comrade in the heat of battle, watching men blown to pieces as the cannons thundered, ripping cloth and flesh to shreds.

The years had become a cruel and utterly merciless business of struggling to stay alive when all of the odds were against it; of watching men die and wondering why it was that fate had spared him when so many had been killed on either side of him. Now, it was all over. But the war had not ended for most of the men in grey, the men who still persisted in wearing the uniform of the Confederate Army. Inwardly too, he was changed. His mind was tight-twisted, knotted with a curiously growing hate which, at the moment, he could not begin to understand. During the fighting, it had not been possible to hate the enemy. They were a strangely nebulous entity that existed only as fleeting shadows, sometimes outlined in brief silhouette against the flashes of the exploding shells, sometimes heard crashing through the brush. But it was not until the war had ended and the uneasy peace had begun, that the enemy had become a personalised being, something on which he could focus his hatred.

He grew aware that the small talk in the saloon had stopped. For a moment, there was a warning tingle along his spine, a sensation that he had learned, from past experience, never to ignore. There was the feel of danger here; if not directed at him, it was very close to him. He forced himself to stare at the bartender and ignore it.

'Whiskey,' he said tightly.

'Sure.' The other nodded curtly, pulled the bottle from under the counter and poured the amber liquid into a glass, setting it in front of him.

'You look surprised.' Devrin murmured after a brief

pause. He glanced at the other over the rim of his glass, locking his gaze with the other man's. 'You got somethin' on your mind?'

'No. Nothin'.' The other shook his head, wet his lips with the tip of his tongue. 'Just that we don't see men still wearin' that colour, even here.'

Devrin smiled thinly, drained his glass and set it down on the bar in front of him. He did not once remove his keen-eyed gaze from the bartender's face.

'I see. Trouble is that I happen to like this colour. If you got any objection I reckon I'd like to hear it.'

The bartender clearly considered himself to be a tough case, and there was a scattergun reposing just beneath the counter within easy reach of his right hand, but something about this man who watched him so closely prompted him to stay his hand. He wilted visibly under Devrin's stare.

'No objections,' he said hoarsely. 'Though it might not be wise to ride around town dressed like that. There are some here who don't like to be reminded of grey.'

'Guess they're too sensitive,' Devrin said. He picked up the bottle and poured another drink.

'Could be they've got a good reason to be.' The other pulled the wet cloth from the belt around his middle and proceeded to wipe the counter. 'Weren't much actual fighting around these parts, but Quantrill and his raiders did plenty of damage, killed some folk, too, close by.'

Devrin nodded. So that was it. At the battlefront, they had heard something of these irregulars who had pillaged the small towns and settlements here; but then they had only been rumours. Now he was coming face to face with the reality and it came to him for the first time how these people must really feel.

'Can I get a meal here?' he asked abruptly, changing the subject.

The other shrugged, hesitated, and Devrin saw his gaze

flick momentarily over his shoulder, as though seeking someone out in the middle of the saloon, looking for guidance. Whatever he was seeking, the answer must have been reassuring and in the affirmative, for he grinned faintly, and said: 'It won't be as good as the meal you'd get in the hotel next door if you cared to wait for a couple of hours until five o'clock, but if you're hungry, I can fix you up with a bite to eat.'

'What you got here?'

'Sowbelly, potatoes, beans, coffee.'

'All right. Fry somethin' up. I'll just arrange for a bed for tonight at the hotel. I'll be back in ten minutes.' Finishing his drink, he slid a couple of coins across the bar. The other's hand snaked out, the fingers closing over the money. Then it was whisked out of sight beneath the soiled apron.

He went rapidly out of the saloon, acutely aware of the eyes of the men at the tables watching him, cast a sudden backward glance at them as he reached the door, pushing it open with the flat of his hand. As one man, they turned their heads and looked away; all except for one of them who sat at a table by himself. He kept his amused glance fixed on Devrin until the other passed through the doors, letting them swing shut behind him.

He had ridden into Fenton on one or two occasions before going to the war, but he recalled little about the town. He had never been inside the hotel here and was surprised to find that it had been freshly painted and newly decorated. He felt a wry grimace twist his lips as he walked along the small lobby to the counter at the far end, eyeing the pimply-faced clerk with a feeling of distaste. Fenton would be getting ready to welcome the hordes of business men from the North who would descend on this country like locusts, parasites, seeking to bleed the State white. But as yet, there was little sign of this.

'I'd like a room, just for the one night,' Devrin told the clerk.

The other laid down the newspaper he had been reading, gave Devrin a hard glance, eyes widening a shade as he saw the tattered uniform which the other wore. Then his gaze flicked to Devrin's face, locked momentarily with the hard stare which the other laid on him and he got swiftly to his feet, scraping back his chair in his hurry to stand up.

'That will be four dollars,' he said, 'including evening meal and breakfast tomorrow morning.'

'Four dollars!' grunted Devrin.

'That's right.' There was a faintly amused smile on the edges of the other's lips. 'Afraid that this is the only hotel in town right now. It'll be another couple of months before they have the other two ready for guests.'

'So until that happens, you're chargin' the sky for a room'

The clerk gave a negligent shrug of his shoulders. Evidently he considered that he was on fairly sure ground. He had taken in everything about the man who stood in front of him. A man used to violence, but one who would not want to spend the night in one of the flea-ridden hovels on the outskirts of the town, the only other alternative to staying at the hotel and paying the fancy prices they charged.

'All right, I'll take it.' Carefully, Devrin counted out four dollars and laid them on the counter in front of the other. The clerk's smile broadened a little as he spun the register and handed the quill pen over to Devrin. When the other had signed his name, he glanced down quickly at it, but it evidently meant nothing to him for he immediately turned and took a key from the wooden rack on the wall behind him.

'Room Fourteen,' he said, pointing to the flight of stairs

that led up to the upper floor. 'You'll find it at the end of the corridor, at the top of the stairs.'

'Thanks.' Devrin nodded. Making his way up the stairs, past the potted plants which lined the stairway, he walked quickly along the corridor, unlocked the door at the far end and stepped inside, glancing about him. The room was clean, sparsely furnished. Going over to the window, he glanced outside, looking down into the street. It was the time of day when the heat head was at the peak of its piled-up intensity and there were few people abroad in the street. Most of them preferred to sit on the boardwalks in the shade of the overhangs, or in the saloons.

He dumped his bag on the chair beside the bed, glanced inside the tall pitcher on the small bureau, discovered it to be full of water and poured half of it into the basin. Stripping off his shirt, he knocked most of the white dust from it, washed his face and chest, feeling the hard mask of caked dirt crack as the water dissolved it, the soap burning his skin with a sharp touch. He had not realised that it had been so hot a day on board that train.

He dried himself with the rough towel, put his shirt back on, feeling a little more fresh than before. The gnawing of hunger in his belly reminded him how long it was since he had eaten. Buckling on his battle-dulled sword and the heavy pistol around his waist, he went down into the lobby, handed over his key, and returned to the saloon.

The meal was waiting for him as he walked in. From behind the bar, the bartender indicated the table near the wall. Nodding, Devrin went over and lowered himself thankfully into the chair, stretching his legs out straight in front of him beneath the table. His appetite was keen now and he ate ravenously, chewing his food, washing it down with the scalding hot coffee. It had been well cooked and he guessed that they were used to providing meals here, considering the hours and prices available at the hotel nearby.

He had just finished the meal, mopping up the last of the rich brown gravy with the bread, when a shadow fell across the table. Glancing up, he stared at the man who had approached cat-footed, now standing near the other chair.

'Mind if I sit down?' asked the other, indicating the vacant chair.

Devrin hesitated. At the moment he was in no real mood for company, yet there was something about the other that made his presence felt. He recognised the other at once as the man who had been so interested in him when he had walked out of the saloon on his way to the hotel. 'Suit yourself,' he said shortly.

The other sat down, eyed him closely for a long moment before speaking, then said quietly. 'Noticed you come in off the train. You looking for a job, or just on your way through?'

'Just moving on,' Lee said harshly. 'I'll be riding out tomorrow.'

'I see.' The other sounded disappointed. 'I was hoping you might be willing to take employment with me. I'm Carl Marsden. I own the Triple Z spread, ten miles west of town. I need good men and I pay good wages.'

'Sorry.' Devrin shook his head. 'I'm still riding out.'

'Sixty a month and all found,' said the other persuasively.

In spite of himself, Lee whistled softly under his breath. This was more than twice what a rider could expect at most of the ranches. And it had seemed to him, from what he had been able to see from the train on his way here, that there was plenty of poverty around in this part of the territory. How could a man like this pay such wages unless he wanted something more than a rider to watch the herd and help around the spread?

'Won't you think it over?' said the other, leaning forward, resting his weight on his elbows.

Lee's smile was thin, his lips stretched tight. 'It seems pretty plain to me, Mister Marsden, that you're not looking for a rider but for somebody who's handy with a gun, and willing to kill if you give the order and ask no questions. I've seen enough killing during the war to last me a lifetime. 1 want no more of it.'

'Now who said anything about killing,' put in the other mildly. He sounded vaguely astonished at the suggestion. Sitting back in his chair he built himself a smoke, waited until it was shaped and alight, then blew a cloud of smoke at the ceiling, his eyes partly closed and went on: 'You've been away from here for a long time. You don't know how things are shaping here. Pretty soon they'll have a big railhead built here and there'll be cattle pens with the buyers moving in from north and east. When that happens I want to be first there with my beef. There'll be a tremendous market for good beef cattle, but it will be those who're first with good, fat cattle, who'll make the killing as far as the best prices are concerned.'

'If that's the case, then I figure you ought to have little difficulty in getting men to work for you, Mister Marsden,' Lee said pointedly. 'Especially considering the wages you seem to be paying.'

'That isn't the point,' Marsden scowled. 'I need a special kind of man. A man I can trust. You think the other ranchers haven't got the same ideas that I have.'

'Maybe so.' Devrin gave him a tough glance. 'But I'm riding home. Could be that if things there don't turn out as I hope, I may come riding back this way and take up your offer. '

'That your last word?'

Devrin nodded tersely. There was something that did not quite add up about Marsden, but at the moment he could not lay his finger on it. The other was too self-confident, seemed to believe that he had only to crook his little finger, offer these high wages and every man would come running to do his bidding. With an effort, he forced down his sudden surge of anger. It was not like him to pre-judge a man before he got to know him better, yet on many such occasions, he had found that his first impressions were usually the correct ones.

Marsden sat watching him for a moment longer, then pushed back his chair, got to his feet and moved away without a backward glance. Going over to the bar, he whispered something to the bartender, then strode out of the saloon. Devrin sat quite still, watching the barkeep out of the corner of his eye. He guessed that the other had been ordered to keep an eye on him, report back everything to Marsden. He felt briefly annoyed, then pushed the feeling away into the background of his mind.

Things had changed a lot since he had ridden out of this territory to fight in the war. Maybe too, he had changed in several small, subtle ways. He knew it would be wrong to expect everything to stand still. There had to be progress and from all accounts, the town was growing, and growing fast. But he could not forget that he had fought a war with these men from the north, men who were now moving in as conquerors, demanding and taking. For the first time, he began to wonder what he might find back home when he rode up to the ranch.

An hour after daylight, he saddled up and returned to the trail, travelling steadily west, the trail winding into higher ground. The heat began to rise as soon as the sun commenced its steady climb to the noon zenith and he was glad by the time he reached the small creek that ran bubbling down the rocky hillside, splashed across the trail and continued on down into the vast flatness of the desert that stretched clear to the southern horizon. Now he was able to pick out well-remembered landmarks. Each one of them was associated with a memory in his mind, bringing back a little of the days before the war when it had been good to set out on the trail at daybreak and ride until the sun was high in the cloudless heavens, returning just as it went down in a flame of scarlet and crimson behind the purple hills on the skyline.

He felt the water brush against his mount's chest as he forded the stream. It had a gravelly bed and there was no danger of the horse losing its footing. The trappings of his saddle were worn and old, but the horse was a thorough-bred, used to hard travel. Once on the far side of the creek, he turned off the trail, climbed up into the tall, sky-reaching pines that grew thickly on both sides of the road. Deep among the trees, with the sharply aromatic smell of the pines in his nostrils, the soft feel of the thick layer of several years of needles underfoot, he rode slowly, savouring each minute of the ride. The red trunks of the trees grew straight and tall and there was scarcely any under-brush among them. The roots were buried deep in the soft soil, and in the pale green light that shafted through the overhead canopy of leaves he found everything so calm and restful that he was almost sad when he finally rode out into the sunlight again, cutting across long looping ridges where the hills shouldered down close to the narrow game run which he followed. He could just make out the wider stretch of the road below him, dusty and grey against the greener background.

Except for the faint metallic jingle of the harness there was no sound to be heard. The intense silence pressed down on him from the high crests of the hills, thick and deep so that he could almost touch it. Once or twice, he rode over a narrow cattle trail which he did not remember from the old days and there was a wide slide that blocked off part of the game run when he was halfway down from the hills, cutting into the wider valley that lay spread out in front of him.

Around the bend, he knew he would come in sight of the ranch for the first time and in spite of himself, a faint tingle of excitement coursed through him. His fingers gripped the reins a little more tightly than necessary. Now, though, he travelled without haste. Far back up north, when he had first left on this long journey back, he had felt the desire for haste burning in him, but it had gradually lessened as the miles had diminished. Now he had developed an inner patience that smothered the urgency.

After the first quick descent, the trail began to degenerate into a series of short breaks where short-grass meadows were interspersed with benches of bare, grey rock. He was not far from the road now and he was very close to the opening into the valley. Another three miles and he would be home. He touched spurs to his horse's flanks and then hesitated as he caught the faint run of another horse in the distance, far-off, but coming closer at a swift run. Interest and caution rose together in his mind. They had been a small community before he had left this valley, small and close-knit. This might be one of them, he decided. Anyway, there was no point in hurrying. He sat quite still in the saddle, following the course of the unseen rider while he built himself a cigarette.

He smoked it slowly, letting the smoke drift from his nostrils in twin streams. Five minutes later, sound and rider came around the bend in the trail together and he eyed the other with sudden interest. The man saw him at once, reined up sharply so that the horse almost threw him. But he was evidently an experienced horseman and swiftly had the animal under control. Leather squealed momentarily. Then the other's voice came at him, slow and easy.

'Howdy. Didn't expect to meet anybody on this stretch of the trail.' His gaze touched on Devrin's grey uniform, but he made no further comment, instead he sat waiting for the other to speak.

'Used to be a well-used trail when I knew it some years ago,' Lee said casually.

He saw the other's eyes narrow swiftly for a moment and a gust of expression go over his features. The sunlight threw its sharp highlights on his face, emphasising the high cheek bones and the deep-set eyes. 'You used to live around here before the war?' It was more of a statement than a question, but Devrin nodded in reply.

'That's right. Riding back now. I suppose some things will have changed, but out here, away from the towns, there can't have been much and—'

He paused as he saw the change come over the stranger's face. It was hard to assess what the change might portend. Quite suddenly and without any real reason, he felt a stab of fear at his stomach.

'There's been some big changes,' said the other slowly. He walked his mount forward until he came level with Devrin. 'Could be it might help if I knew your name.'

'Lee Devrin. My family have the ranch about three miles from here.'

'Devrin.' The other's expression was evidence that he knew the name, although Lee did not recognise him even now when he saw him close to. 'And you're just riding back from the war'?'

Devrin sucked in a sharp gust of air, let it out in slow, measured pinches. 'You've got something on your mind, mister,' he said tightly, lips thinned. 'I'd be obliged if you'd tell me what it is.'

For a long moment, the other stared at him, a strange look in his eyes. Then he said slowly. 'I've got some real bad news for you, son. I never figured that anybody would come riding back. Didn't know your folks personally, of course. I didn't come out here until a little over a year ago. It happened about ten months before that, I reckon.'

'What happened? What is it you've trying to say?' Almost without being aware of it, he had leaned sideways, grasping the other's arm, his fingers biting in through the rough cloth of the other's sleeve with a steel-like strength. But if the other felt the tight-fingered grip he gave no outward sign. He had something to tell him and the telling of it was evidently not going to be easy.

There was a tightness laid around the stranger's mouth as he said: 'Your folks are dead, son. They've been dead for nigh on a year and a half.'

'Dead!' For several moments the single word meant absolutely nothing to him. His mind seemed to be numb and he fumbled around in his thought striving to realise the full enormity of what the other had said. Death for him meant only the bloody mutilation of what he had seen on the field of battle, nothing else, an unclean thing which could never be associated with his family. He tried to imagine his mother and father, his sister in the same terrible postures as the companions who had been killed in the tangled ugliness of the Wilderness, but nothing came to mind.

He sat wholly still in the saddle as the other told him of the night when Quantrill's Raiders had swooped down on the peaceful valley, bringing fire and death with them. As he listened, his lips stretched thin across his face and a tiny muscle began to twitch high in his cheek. On the reins, his fingers tightened convulsively and his eyes changed, opening fully on the other with a look that the man could not understand, could not even begin to comprehend. At the moment though, it seemed to Clem Danaher that the other actually hated him for this, that any anger and hatred which he felt was temporarily transferred from the men who had been responsible to the man who had to tell him this news.

'You have any idea where any of these men are now?' Devrin asked. He was all tight and closed up. His mind felt numbed yet, his skull a shell for an aching emptiness.

'Scattered – all of 'em,' the other said softly. 'It was a long time ago and a lot has happened since then.' Devrin nodded slowly. His mind told him that the question had been a foolish and superfluous one. Of course the other would know very little, if anything. As he had said, it had all happened before he had come to the valley himself, but there had to be somebody in the neighbourhood who knew something, who might know the identity of even one of these men. If he could only find one of them he would be able to force the rest of the information he needed out of him. The thought gave him a momentary, sadistic pleasure. But the feeling faded swiftly.

He said: 'What would they want to kill innocent men and women for? They weren't soldiers. They couldn't be any danger to them.'

'Quantrill didn't need no excuse to go murdering and plundering,' said the other thinly. 'He just went out and did it.' A pause, then he went on a trifle more slowly, his tone still serious. 'I know how you must feel, son.'

'Do you?' said Devrin bitterly.

'I reckon so.' The other nodded his head. 'I'm on my way into Fenton. I have a small place just on the far side of the valley. My daughter's there now. If you'd care to ride on over and tell her I sent you, I'm sure she'll get you a bite to eat and then you and I could talk things over this evening when I get back.'

'Is there anything more you can tell me about all this?' asked Devrin pointedly,

'Perhaps. I can also ask around town. If you was to do that and any of those men who rode with Quantrill are still

41

around, you might scare 'em off. But nobody would take much notice of me.'

Lee drew in his breath; let it out again more slowly. 'Then I'll thank you for your hospitality, Mister – '

'Clem Danaher,' said the other. He extended his hand. 'Mary will see that you get something to eat. And you're welcome to stay with us for as long as you like.'

Numbly, Devrin watched as the other rode off. Then he wheeled his mount sharply, raked spurs along its flanks and rode swiftly into the valley. He urged the horse forward until he came upon the blackened ruins that stood in the small square of trampled, sun-baked earth which had once been the courtyard of the ranch.

Reining up, he sat for a long while, feeling the stillness grow about him, the curious tightness in his chest, and the painful bunching of his stomach muscles. He sat for so long that after a while the horse turned its head to regard him curiously.

Softly, he said: 'Maybe you're right, fella. Time we rode on and put all of this behind us.'

He moved up the trail, through a narrow gulch, out into the second valley that opened off from the first, smaller, but still full of lush green grass. The evening's coolness was still a long way off and he wiped the sweat from his forehead as it began to trickle into his eyes. There was a small ranch house set near the base of the low, rolling hills a mile or so away and he guessed that this was Danaher's spread. He turned the horse towards it, reining up fifteen minutes later in front of the porch. There was a pause and then the door opened and a girl stepped out on to the veranda. Tall and slim, he recognised her as the girl who had got off the train the previous day in Fenton.

# FURY!

Mary Danaher watched him as he finished the last of the gravy, wiping it up with his bread until the plate was clean. There was something about this man which intrigued her, something more than the uniform he wore even though it was that of the defeated Army, more than the fact that his name was Devrin and that his family had been killed, his home destroyed while he had been away at the war. His face seemed so brown in the sunlight which streamed through the windows, his eyes so piercing in their direct intensity. There was the feeling in her mind that he was a loner. A man who rode a lonely trail, driven on by something he could not even begin to fathom himself, some driving force that set him aside from other men. Maybe it was the news which her father had broken to him.

She flushed a little at her own thoughts as she turned back to the stove and picked up the coffee pot, walking back to the table and pouring him out a cup. He spooned sugar into it, poured in some of the condensed milk from the tin, then sipped it slowly. His eyes lifted to hers.

Embarrassed, she said quickly: 'I'm sorry that you should have to ride back and discover that this had happened. There were a lot of things that went on during the war that decent people abhorred.'

His lips thinned for a moment, then he set down his

half-empty cup. 'I've got nothing against the soldiers who fought in the war. I killed men myself. But this is different. This was nothing but sheer, cold-blooded murder. These men were not even soldiers. They pillaged and looted the homes of innocent folk who had no direct part in the war. They followed no code at all.'

She dropped her eyes out of pity, tightened her entwined fingers in her lap as she sat there at the table. 'What do you intend to do now? All of this happened so long ago that the sheriff back in town won't take any action, even if you were to ask him. There were others killed by these irregulars and just after the war finished, some people tried to get them brought to justice, but the law refused to have warrants sworn out. The trouble was that most of these killers have important posts in the administration now. The Northerners are moving in and taking everything they can lay their hands on. We're a defeated country now. They feel that as conquerors they can have the spoils of war even though the war has been over for almost a year.'

'1 saw a little of that in town,' he said bitterly. 'I know better than to try to have these men brought to justice by the law. There is no justice as far as that is concerned.'

'Then what do you have in mind? Try to start the ranch all over again? Somehow I doubt if you'd get your land back. Somebody from the North is almost sure to have staked a claim to it and by the time you try to get it settled in some court of law, it will be too late.'

'Getting the land back doesn't really interest me at the moment,' he said, his voice very soft, deceptively mild. 'If there's no justice in this part of the territory, then I intend to carry it out myself.'

'You're going to go after these men?'

He nodded. 'I'll find them if it's the last thing 1 do.'

'And when you do?'

'Then I'll kill them just as they killed my folk.'

She ignored his anger. 'But how will you find them? It all happened so long ago and—'

'Somehow, I'll find the name of one of them and when I reach him, he'll tell me everything else I want to know.'

She shook her head, her face filled with a strange softness. For a moment there was sadness in her expression. 'I know how badly this news must have hit you. But is it worth all of the trouble, the danger? You'll hunt and you'll fight and you won't know any rest at all until you've finished this, or die in the attempt. The only thing that will drive you on will be your desire for revenge, to balance the books against your parents.'

'What else would you have a man do?' He looked at her directly, his eyes snapping at her from beneath the straight-drawn brows.

'I don't know. I suppose it's because nothing like this ever happened to me so I find it hard to put myself in your place. I guess I might do the same as you're wanting to do.'

'Your father said he'd ask around in town to see if he could find out anything. Said he'd be back this evening. When do you expect him?'

'Are you all that anxious to get started on this trail of vengeance?' Now there was a definite beat of scepticism and bitterness in her tone.

'No, but I'd like to know just where I stand in this thing. I figured that when the war finished, it would mean the end of fighting and killing as far as I was concerned. I wanted nothing more out of life than to ride home and take up where I left off. Now it seems that all this is changed, that none of it is to be. So I have to adjust my thoughts and actions.'

She bent her head for a moment, then got to her feet. 'I'll get the dishes washed,' she said sharply. 'I expect Dad should be home around seven o'clock.'

She went through into the kitchen and he heard her with the dishes, clattering them in the sink. She was angry, but because of his growing bitterness he found it hard to see why.

Lee Devrin stood on the porch, resting his shoulder against the two-by-two upright, staring off to the east, to where the small valley narrowed and the humped rocks crowded it out. It was late evening and the sun had gone down a little over an hour before, throwing the dark shadows over the country. He could smell the strong scent of the mesquite that grew in tight little bunches among the grass. He had his mind wholly on the news he had learned that day and as yet he felt no concern for Danaher, although the other was now almost two hours overdue.

Turning at a sudden sound behind him, he saw the girl come out of the house, a worried look on her face. She came over and stood beside him, looking off into the darkness.

'He should have been back before now,' she said tightly. 'I think something may have happened to him.'

'Could be he stopped in town to have a drink with a few friends,' Devrin said. 'There are a host of reasons why he's late.'

'But he's always been so punctual. He knows that I worry about him if he doesn't get back when he says he will.'

'You forget that he promised he'd try to get some information for me while he was in town.'

She nodded, but was obviously not entirely convinced. 'That wouldn't have taken all this time. And it's because he's going around asking these questions that I feel sure something is wrong.'

Lee dropped the butt of his cigarette into the dust and

ground it out under his heel. He felt a trifle uncomfort-
able, knowing that inwardly the girl was blaming him for
this. Finally, he said: 'Would you like me to ride back a way
and take a look-see?'

'Would you?' she asked. 'I'd feel a lot easier in my mind
if you would. In fact, I'll saddle up and ride with you. Just
sitting here, not knowing, would be too much for me.'

'All right. If that's what you want to do.' He shrugged,
stepped over to the small corral, whistled up his horse,
slapped the saddle on it, then did the same for the other
horse.

Five minutes later, they rode out from the ranch heading towards the narrow pass. Lee said nothing to the girl
as they rode. Depression and obvious apprehension had
dampened her spirit and he could see that she was struggling with her innermost thoughts, striving to convince
herself that nothing was wrong, that she was merely exag-
gerating everything in her mind, connecting incidents
and forming them into a possibility which could be very
far from the truth. She rode with her eyes fixed ahead, her
lips set firmly together, compressed tightly. The talk they
had had earlier had clearly left her still displeased with
him, but there was more on her mind than this.

They reached the further valley, rode in silence past the
burnt-out ruins of the houses and barns which stood a
little way back from the trail. In spite of the tight grip he
had on himself, Lee felt the cold finger of tension trace a
line up and down his spine.

Deliberately he averted his glance as they rode past.
Soon they reached timber and came upon the trail that
wound down through the heavily-wooded slopes. Out of
the corner of his eye, he watched Mary Danaher as she sat
tall and straight, rather like a man, in the saddle. Once, he
noticed her turn her head to look round at him, as though
a sudden thought had struck her and she was on the point

of saying something, but she obviously thought better of it, and remained silent.

They came to the more rocky country that lay beyond the timberline and for the first time, Lee began to feel a little apprehensive about Clem Danaher. When they had ridden out from the ranch, he had been quite confident that they would meet up with the other somewhere along the trail within half an hour or so of leaving. But they had been riding for more than an hour now without coming across any sign of him.

The girl reined up as they came out on to a wide, flat bench of rock from which they were able to look down on the trail that ran like a twisting scar through the darker background of the terrain. She said quietly, evidently keeping her emotions under tight control. 'What do you think now? If he left town at his usual time, he should have got much further than this.'

'Has he ever been known to stay the night in town?'

'Never.' The girl's tone was emphatic. 'He knows I would be out at the ranch alone through the night.'

'I guess you're right,' Lee said, puzzled. 'Let's move on a little way and take a look down there. It could be that—' He broke off sharply, caught the girl's wrist. The sound of an approaching horse came out of the stillness ahead of them. He said, very slowly, 'This could be him. But don't make a move until you're sure. There seems to be something mighty funny going on around here.'

'Something moving down there,' whispered the girl. She raised a hand and pointed.

Lee strained his vision, pushing his sight through the darkness. He made out the movement, saw the horse come into sight around a bend in the trail, saw instantly that it was riderless.

'Let's get down there,' he said sharply. He spurred his own mount forward, down on to the wide trail. The riderless horse shied away from him as he came up to it, but he managed to swing down and catch at the reins. A moment later Mary Danaher came up to him. She uttered a startled cry as she recognised the horse.

'That's my father's horse,' she said harshly. 'Something has happened! He's probably been killed somewhere along the trail and—'

'Steady on there,' Lee said tautly. He released his hold on the reins and caught the girl's shoulder, shaking her roughly, hoping to evoke a shock response. 'There could be some other explanation. We'd better backtrack and see if we can find any sign of him. It's not going to be easy in this darkness but the moon should be coming up soon and that ought to give us plenty of light to see by.'

Twenty minutes onward they came to a narrow canyon that cut a dark sliver of shadow through the rocks. The moon had lifted now above the looming ridge above them and flooded the scene with light, except where the deep midnight shadow lay across the narrow slash of the canyon floor.

Hauling up his mount, Lee pointed to the dusty ground directly in front of them. 'Plenty of prints here,' he said. 'Judging from the way they was milling around, I'd say this is where it happened.'

He dismounted, went forward a little way and bent, examining the ground closely, running his fingers over it as he tried to read the sign in the dimness of it lifting into the air about him, soaking through his clothing. The chill of it continued to rise to him as he edged forward, every sense alert for the first sign of trouble. They had, as yet, no way of telling how long ago this had happened. It could have been an hour or only a few minutes. There was a break at the very edge of the trail and he shuffled his feet until he reached it; got down on to his knees and peered forward into the blackness, still not sure of what he saw.

He sat back for a moment drawing in a long breath, then he reached forward with his fingers until they encountered nothing. Picking up a small piece of rock, he let it go over the side, heard it strike once on the way down and then splash into the water.

It was better than a six-foot drop down there, he decided finally. He was on the point of edging away when he heard the faint sound from almost immediately below him.

Turning, he called softly: 'Mary! Over here! Quickly.' Less than ten seconds later, she was crouched beside him. 'What is it?'

'I think your father is down there. I'm going to try to find a way down to him. It may be a sheer drop but that's a chance I have to take.'

Cautiously, he turned and lowered himself over the lip of rock, feeling desperately for toeholds in the solid rock-face. For several seconds his feet swung helplessly, finding nothing. Then he managed to dig in his toes into a small niche, holding his legs at full strength while he slowly lowered all of his weight on to them. Bracing himself, he felt around, moving downward, clutching tightly at the roots which grew out of the rock.

'Are you all right?' The girl's concerned whisper floated down to him from the dimness.

'I think so,' he murmured back. The strain in his arms and shoulders was beginning to make itself felt. His face was sticky and there was the taste of salt on his lips, the sweat dripping into his eyes as it worked its way from beneath the drooping brim of his hat. Anchoring himself with both legs, he kicked at the rock, hoping to dig himself a foothold. But his boots seemed to make no impression on it at all.

Arms taking the strain from the insecure foothold, he slithered down the side of the cutting, arms and knees scraping the rough surface. Finally, he hit the bottom with a jar that knocked all of the air out of his lungs. For a while, he lay there, sucking air into his lungs, gathering his strength. At length, he managed to push himself on to his hands and knees, peering about him as he tried to make out the injured man. He found the other a few moments later, lying with his back against the rocks, legs thrust out in front of him. The other's face was glistening wet and streaked with dust and sweat.

'Danaher?' Lee muttered softly.

A pause, then the other answered 'Who's that?'

'Lee Devrin. Your daughter and I came out looking for you when you didn't turn up at the ranch. Seems to me it was a good thing we did, otherwise you'd have lain here all night. How badly are you hurt?'

'It's my leg,' gritted the other through tightly-clenched teeth. He was holding his thigh and Lee noticed that he was rocking the injured leg slowly from side to side as though in an effort to ease the agony.

'Better let me take a look at it.' Lee reached forward, touched the other's leg, felt the warm stickiness of blood on the man's trousers, just above the knee.

'A couple of coyotes jumped me along the trail,' muttered the other, wincing as Lee explored the wound. 'Shot me in the leg. My horse bolted and they came after me. I managed to crawl into the rocks, but went over the edge here.'

'Lucky you weren't killed outright, falling from up there.'

'Reckon so.' He glanced up at Lee. 'Where's Mary now? Back at the ranch?'

'No. She insisted on riding out with me. She's up there now.'

Danaher sighed. He drew in a shuddering breath, began to moan and move his leg again.

'Better try to hold still,' Lee told him. 'You'll only start the bleeding again and it looks as if you've lost a lot of blood already. I'll try to get you up there and back to the ranch. We'll get a doctor out to take a look at you.'

'Don't need a doctor,' gasped the other. 'The bullet went all the way through which ain't so bad. Besides, they'll be watching out for you, and for Mary, if you rode back into Fenton.'

'Then hold still and I'll try to bind it up for you. Somehow, we've got to get you back on to the trail.'

'How'd you know I was down here?' muttered the other, his tone pulsing with pain.

'We ran into your horse a ways back along the trail, guessed you were somewhere around. Then we found the spot where other horses had been milling around and decided to scout the trail.'

'Lucky for me that you did,' gritted the other. He sucked in a sharp gust of air as Lee shifted his leg slightly, wrapping his kerchief tightly around the wound. There was a neat hole where the bullet had gone in, but it had torn the flesh appreciably on the way out and it was here that most of the bleeding had occurred.

A few moments later, the girl's voice reached them, drifting down from the darkness above their heads. 'Have you found him yet, Lee?'

'He's down here, Mary,' Devrin called back. 'A bullet wound in the leg. It's not too bad. but he's lost quite a lot of blood and the sooner we get him back to the ranch the better.'

'Shouldn't we ride with him into town and let Doc Beaudry take a look at it? It's twice as far back to the ranch and he could lose his leg if it becomes infected.'

'No, Mary. We've got to make it back to the ranch.' Clem Danaher spoke before Lee could open his mouth to reply. 'Don't waste time asking too many questions. Just believe me and do as I say.'

'All right, Father.' The girl's tone was little more than a husky whisper, puzzled, but accepting what the other said without question.

Moving forward, Lee caught the wounded man by the shoulders and gently eased him to his feet. 'Try not to put too much weight on that leg of yours,' he said tautly. 'I'll try to help you up. Think you can manage it all right?'

'Sure, I'll be okay,' muttered the other through tightly clenched teeth. 'I don't want to hurry you, but those critters who did this might come riding back to be sure they did the job right.'

Devrin nodded. That was something which had not occurred to him, but it seemed a reasonable assumption to make. Evidently Danaher had discovered something in town which these men did not want spread around and they had done their best to make sure he remained permanently silent.

Bracing himself, he lifted the other up the rock face, felt the shudder of agony that went through Danaher's body, then heard his fingers scrabbling for a handhold in the rock. A moment later, the other said harshly. 'There's a root here that should bear my weight. I'm going to try to pull myself up.'

Another movement further up told Lee that the girl had shifted her position and was leaning down to help her father. Between them, they succeeded in getting the other on to the rocky ground at the lip of the trail. Less than two minutes later, Devrin was up, lying flat on his stomach for a moment, getting his wind back, rubbing his chest where the sharp edge of rock had scraped it as he had wormed his way over.

Wind scoured along the narrow canyon where it acted as a natural funnel, and he felt the chill coldness on his back and face where the sweat had congealed on his flesh.

His face was sticky and when he took off his hat for a moment, sweat dripped down into his eyes from the sweat-band. Somewhere in the night there were other sounds which he could not identify, rising and falling, fading away and then coming across to them again. He halted for a moment and listened intently. Somewhere men were riding but it was impossible to say in which direction. At night, with all of the stillness around, hearing was the most deceptive of the senses. Most likely they were echoes carried along by the nearby creek, he reflected.

'You think those could be the same men?' murmured Mary Danaher, stepping close to him, her head cocked a little on one side.

'Could be,' he muttered non-committally. 'Whether they are or not, the sooner we get out of here, the better.'

He turned to the man nearby. 'Reckon you could manage to stay in the saddle, Clem?'

'Sure.' The other's face was a pale grey blur in the faint moonlight that filtered down among the rocks. 'If you could just help me into the saddle.'

Danaher's horse still stood patiently nearby against the boulders. Helping him into the saddle, Lee watched for a moment until he was certain the other could hold on, then went back to his own mount, swung up into the saddle and led the way out of the canyon.

It was almost midnight when they rode into the courtyard, dismounted and turned their horses loose into the corral. Together, Lee and the girl helped Danaher into the house and while the girl lit the lantern on the table, Lee eased the other into one of the chairs, then cut a slit in the leg of his trousers with his knife, exposing the wound a couple of inches above the knee. There had been only a little fresh bleeding and he gave a satisfied nod as he looked down at it.

'He'll do,' he said to the girl. To Danaher, he said: 'You're going to have a stiff leg for a while, but that's all. I'll clean it up and then put on a fresh bandage. After that, I figure you'd better get some sleep.'

'Don't you want to know what I found out in town?'

Lee lifted his head to find the other's gaze fixed on him intently. He ran the tip of his tongue around his lips, then said: 'It can wait until morning, I reckon. Unless you particularly want to get it off your mind.'

Danaher laid his glance on Lee like the edge of a knife, motionless, but ready to cut. His lips crept nearer together as Devrin cleaned the wound, then wrapped the linen around it. There was an odd tightness on his face which Lee had not seen before.

'After what happened to me tonight, I'm undecided whether to tell you or not. These men evidently are afraid of you, otherwise they wouldn't have tried to stop me from telling you. When they find out that their attempt was unsuccessful, they'll come after you. So I figure it'd be better for you to know everything. That way, you'll know what you're up against.'

All right.' It was clear to Lee that the other wanted to talk and it might be better for him to get it off his mind. Maybe he would sleep better that way, with a clear conscience.

'There's a man in town called Bassard. There's been talk in the past that he rode with Quantrill during the raids in this part or the territory. He works for Monaghan, owner of the Double C spread. Foreman there. I guess that if anybody could tell you what you want to know, then Bassard is your man, but it won't be easy to get to him.'

Devrin looked at him, curious. 'You mean that Monaghan protects the men who ride for him?'

'Something like that,' nodded the other. 'These riders stick together closer than flies.'

'And you think it could have been Bassard and some of these men who shot you back there on the trail?'

Danaher shrugged. 'Maybe. It was too dark to recognise any of them. But I can't think of anybody else who'd resent me prying around.'

'No, neither can I,' Lee acknowledged. He got to his feet. 'Maybe I'll take a look around and ask a few questions for myself tomorrow.'

'Be careful,' said Mary Danaher from the doorway. 'These men are evil. They would drive us off the range if they could. They want to grab all of the land and water for themselves and they've managed to get the backing of the law behind them.'

'You mean the law in Fenton?' There was a beat of sarcasm in Lee's voice.

She nodded. 'They ride out here and accuse us of rustling stock from the big ranchers, go through our herds looking for altered brands. So far, they've found nothing. But they'll undoubtedly go on trying until they do pin something on us. When that happens, they'll have an excuse to ride in and take everything.'

Lee nodded. It was an old and familiar situation. The old ways of violence out here along the southern frontiers, never changing, never varying, slowly working their way along the borders. The big men claimed they had the right to all of the land and water, they regarded the smaller folk as intruders, to be fought and destroyed by every means at their disposal, legal or otherwise.

He said: 'Better get some rest now and stay off that leg as much as possible to give it a chance to heal.'

Five minutes later, he stepped out on to the front porch, into the cool night air, rolling himself a smoke. Lighting the cigarette, he drew deeply on it, relishing the bite of the smoke in his throat and lungs. It brought a little of the warmth back into his body. The moon sailed serenely into the cloudless heavens and threw down a cold, eerie light over the hills and small valleys around the ranch. Everything here was so quiet that one could imagine he heard the voice of God speaking out over the stretching wilderness, vibrating softly in the utter silence.

Mary came out of the door, saw him, and walked over, standing beside him. Her face was in shadow as she said softly: 'When you first came here I asked you if you thought it would be wise to rake up the ashes of the past again. I'm still asking you that, especially after what happened to my father. He has no direct concern with this, yet someone tried to kill him. Just think what they will do to you if you start probing around, bringing up the old things that are best forgotten.'

He did not doubt the seriousness of her voice and he could sense the concern she felt for him. But he still experienced the little rise of anger in his mind that anyone should question what he had decided to do. With an effort he fought it down and when he spoke, his tone was quiet and measured.

'Do you honestly think these men are going to let me settle down and live here in peace even if I don't start raking up the past?' He shook his head, gazed down at her upturned face through the slowly drifting tobacco smoke. 'They'd never feel safe themselves. They'd always be wondering what I intend doing and that would be enough to make them want to kill me.'

She gave him a keen glance, arrested by his remark. He could see by the expression on her face that she understood what he was saying. 'I wonder how much you believe that and how much you're motivated by the desire to avenge the death of your family.'

'Maybe they're both linked together in my mind and I'll never be able to separate them,' he agreed. 'But it shouldn't matter to you. Or your father.'

'Don't you consider that we're already implicated?' She leaned her shoulders against the wooden upright. 'My father never really came here with the intention of setting up a ranch like this. He just wanted a place to settle down and put down his roots once the war was over. Then the bigger men began to resent him because they wanted his valley and the water here. Like I said, they tried to run him out, but he wouldn't run and their efforts only made him more stubborn. Now he'll stay here even if they try to kill him as Quantrill and his raiders did to those others a few years ago. I think that inwardly he's unforgiving. Maybe too, he has every right to be. He believes that a man should be free to live his life as he pleases so long as he harms no one else.'

'He'll find that whatever a man does, it always has an effect on someone else. That's the way of things.'

She looked at him with her lips close together, studying him, trying to guess at what went on in his mind, deep below the surface where it never really showed. 'I don't admire your actions, Lee – such as I know them – and I'm sure that you'll only start more bloodshed here, but I doubt if anything I can do or say will make you change your mind.'

'Perhaps it's because you've never seen the evil that I have,' he said softly. 'When you're older, and if things go the way they seem to be right now, you'll see it for yourself and then perhaps you'll understand why a man has to do these things, whether he likes it or not.'

'But do you like to look at life this way? Don't you ever want to fight it?'

'You can only fight evil with its own weapons,' he retorted, grinding out the butt of the cigarette. 'Sometimes you find that it tries to corrupt you. That is the enemy you have to fight.'

She sighed, shook her head. 'I wish I could understand

you, know what it is that's driving you on like this. It can't be just the war, or the fact that you've come home to find your parents dead and everything you knew destroyed.'

'That's a big part of it,' he said.

Silence grew between them, At length, after several minutes, she turned away, clasped her arms about her against the chill, said: 'You won't be able to ride into town in that uniform unless you're really looking for trouble. I think I can find you some clothes that will make you a little less conspicuous.'

She went into the house, letting the door close softly behind her. Lee stood in the still darkness, trying to put his thoughts into some form of order. They were racing chaotically around in his mind as he struggled to form some kind of coherence. Things had been happening to him a little too quickly and unexpectedly for him to take everything in at once.

He knew that the girl's talk was also working through him. Her judgement of him had been based on first impressions, he knew; and it burned in his mind, eating at him like slow acid. For a long while, he let his mind dwell on the easy, simple, uncomplicated events before the war, the thoughts which he had deliberately put away from himself, into the background of his mind. He knew that he was somehow a different man to that youth who had ridden out in the grey uniform all those long, bitter years before, fired with the zeal and desire to fight for what he believed to be right. Now he was embittered by the injustice of the world as he found it and he knew that it was something he could do nothing about. The forces at work here were bigger and more powerful than he was, they could take his poor clay and mould it to their own shapes and forms.

The valley stretched from left to right beneath Devrin's

gaze. In the first rays of the early morning sun, there were long, pointed shadows lying over it, but these were shortening almost visibly as the sun rose from behind the low hills to the east. He selected a deep ravine and rode along its rocky, shadowed course. The horse half slid down into the floor of the high-walled canyon and finally reached the bottom in a shower of small stones and boulders. Halfway along the ravine there was a small cavity where rain water had gathered to form a shallow pool and he dismounted here, let the horse drink its fill while he sat on a flat-topped boulder and smoked a cigarette,

He still was not exactly sure of what he intended to do once he reached Fenton. He had a faint notion that if he kept his eyes and ears open he might learn a lot, especially about this man Bassard who could supply him with some of the information he wanted. He did not doubt that once he located the other, he could make the man talk. During the war, he had often been forced to interrogate captured Union prisoners and he had learned that there were definite limits to the amount of pain that a man could withstand. He had also learned how to apply the methods of torture which would make a man talk more quickly than otherwise, and loosen the most stubborn tongue. He was quite prepared to use such methods again if he had to.

There was the rustle of a lizard as it slithered from one rock to another and out of the corner of his eye he saw the animal come to rest on a boulder a few yards away and regard him unwinkingly in the faint light. It remained poised there for several seconds. and was then gone in a blur of speed and colour as he rose to his feet, went over to the horse and tightened the cinch under its belly before mounting up once more.

They threaded their way in and out of the tall rocks that littered the floor of the canyon. At some time or other in the distant past, a river had run through here, carrying these rocks down as sediment, leaving them high and dry when it had dried up. The narrow, high-walled fissures at the far end had sharp, jagged edges and in places there was only just sufficient room for them to squeeze their way through, the rock tearing at his legs.

By the time the sun was high above the eastern horizon and the shadows were short, they had come out of the ravine and were riding at an easy lope over the vastness of the plain.

After an hour's travel over the dusty wilderness, they moved into the brush-covered slopes at the edge of the plain and he rested the horse again. Long shafts of sunlight lingered their way through the tall trunks of the pines which stood on the slopes of the hills a couple of miles in the distance. As he sat in the saddle, the sombreness of his mood filtered down through into his mind. Even the clothing he now wore reflected his mood, he thought grimily. The wide-brimmed hat that threw a shadow over his forehead and eyes, with a slim rawhide thong under his chin. The leather had been softened and smoothed by long years of a man's thoughtful fingers stroking it he guessed, and this gave him an insight into the kind of man Clem Danaher was; for these were his clothes supplied to him by the girl.

A coyote howled off in the desert, the sound rising and falling along an eerie, saw-toothed scale. In spite of himself, he shivered at the sound. In all the world, he knew of no other noise which held in it such a note of terrible loneliness. The sound ended abruptly on a high chattering note and in the stillness that ensued, he thought he picked out a mournful anxious chorus of high and low notes, drifting towards him on the faint breeze. Leaning forward in the saddle, hooking his fingers over the pommel, he listened intently.

Over there, he figured, there was a bunch of critters

and that meant a ranch spread. It might be the Double C, he reflected idly. If that were so, then he could be riding into danger if he moved off the trail in that direction. The absence of good grazing stock in the area puzzled him for he would have expected a herd to be bedded down on good grass, especially as it would soon be noon and the full heat of the day.

Touching spurs to the horse's flanks, he let his fingertips brush the butt of the revolver in his belt, then moved steadily out of the tree-lined ridges and out on to a broad flat, bare rock in most places, interspersed here and there with tufts of a coarse, hard, wiry grass that was of little use to cattle. Edging forward, he took care not to show himself on the skyline.

# THE VENGEFUL MEN

Beyond the rise lay a shallow basin through which ran a narrow creek and on the far side of the water a small herd was bunched close together in a shifting mass of brown and black. The doleful litany of their bawling was loud now. A couple of riders hemmed the herd close in to the far bank of the creek, one or other of them breaking away now and then to bring back a rebel steer as the animal tried to move off.

Crouching low, Lee watched the scene intently trying to figure out what was going on. It did not seem likely that these cattle had been brought here to graze, yet why were they here then? Were these men shifting them to fresh pastures? Even that did not quite seem to fit. Then he shifted his glance off to his right, saw the small covered wagon that stood on a stretch of high ground perhaps fifty yards away, almost completely hidden by an outcropping of rock. He had missed it with his first sweeping gaze. Now he concentrated his attention on it, saw the two men working near it, smelled the hot stench of burning cowhide drifting on the wind, wrinkling the back of his nostrils. So that was it? Rustlers changing the brands of these critters.

At once, he recalled what Danaher had told him. How

63

Monaghan had tried to accuse the smaller folk of rustling off his cattle, had tried to pin the blame on to them so that he might have an excuse for getting the law at his back and moving in to run the settlers out of the territory. A grim smile played momentarily on his lips as he watched the men at work. Everything was beginning to fit into place now.

Unless he missed his guess, these men were from the Double C spread, running off cattle and then shifting the blame on to others. As far as he could tell there were only the four of them; long odds if he decided to do anything about it, but not too long.

Turning his mount, he rode along the lee of the ridge, approaching the outcrop of rock behind which the wagon was situated. His fingers rested close to the gun in his belt as he came up on top of the ledge. He was now barely ten yards from the two men but both were too intent on their work to even notice him. Then, as though sensing danger, the man holding down the struggling, bawling steer suddenly lifted his head, stared up at Lee, a dark silhouette on the skyline with the sun glaring at the back of him.

The man's sudden hiss of breath was clearly audible. He released his hold on the steer and it threshed its legs convulsively for a moment, before rolling on to its side and staggering to its feet. The bearded man with the branding iron muttered a harsh curse, turned on his companion, then he too stared round at Lee.

His reaction was instinctive and immediate. His hand dropped with the speed of a striking snake for his gun. But it was only half clear of its holster before he froze, found himself staring down the black, circular hole of Lee's pistol.

'Don't try it,' Devrin warned. 'I don't want to have to kill either of you, but I will if you make a move like that again. Now drop that gun back into leather and keep your hand well away from it.'

'I don't know who you are, mister,' snarled the other in a vicious tone. 'Or what you're doin' here, but whatever it is, it's none of your business. So my advice is to ride on.'

'Seems to me that you're doin' a little brandin' of these critters,' Devrin said quietly, leaning forward a little in the saddle, his gun still pointed in the direction of the two men, covering them so that he could aim it at either of them in the twinkling of an eye if they made a wrong move. 'And I don't think it'll make any difference how loud you talk, those other two won't hear you from here.'

He saw by the fractional slump of their shoulders that this was what they had both been banking on.

The bearded one slitted his eyes against the glare of the sun. 'All right, mister, so you've got the drop on us. Suppose you start tellin' us why you're here and what all this is about. I guess you've got to have some reason.'

'Sure,' Devrin said easily. 'I figure that you're Double C riders and that you've been ordered to rustle off these steers and change the brands so that the small ranchers can get the blame.' A quick look at the men's faces convinced him that he had hit the mark with this statement. He saw the way their eyes grew shifty, as they glanced at each other.

'What business is that of yours'?' demanded the taller of the men. 'You a Ranger or somethin' like that?'

'No. Just a citizen who doesn't like to see injustice bein' done.'

The bearded man smiled thinly. He shrugged. 'Then I figure you'd better take that up with the boss, or the foreman. We just take orders. We don't ask any questions, just do like we're told. It's a lot healthier that way. A man gets to live longer.'

'Not if the small ranchers should decide that they've had enough of the crooked lawmen in this territory and take matters into their own hands. If that should happen, you might find it decidedly unhealthy to be around here.'

Both men grinned now, but with a little uncertainty showing through in their eyes. They had been caught at a disadvantage and it was clear that neither had expected him to be as fast with a gun as he was. Now they were evidently busily trying to figure out a way of extricating themselves from this position without exposing themselves to his fire.

'That ain't likely,' grunted the tall man at length. 'Monaghan has this range sewn up pretty tight and the law will back him. Nobody will dare to go against him.'

Devrin was silent for a long moment, letting the pressure of his gaze have its effect on them. Then he said sharply: 'I hear you've got a man named Bassard working at the ranch?'

'Bassard? Sure, he's the foreman.' There was puzzlement in the other's tone. 'What you want him for?'

'Just to ask a few questions. Nothing more.'

The men did not show much surprise. With the least possible grin, the bearded one said: 'You know, I figure that Hague Bassard might want to have a talk with you, mister. He don't like folk askin' questions about him unless they're to his face. But somehow, I reckon he won't want to be at the wrong end of that gun of yours. Guess we may have to do somethin' about that.'

Devrin tightened his lips suddenly. There had been a note of confidence in the man's voice which he had noticed at once, one which he did not like. He sensed danger, just a split second before it came and from the direction he least expected it.

The voice behind him said: 'Drop the gun, mister! Right now!'

Devrin's horse reared at the sudden interruption and he fought it down as the man at his back moved around into sight. There was a rifle in his hands, his finger tight and bar-straight on the trigger. There was no chance at all. For a moment, the thought of action lived in Devrin's mind, but he forced it away. That would have been plain suicide.

Letting go the gun, he dropped it on to the hard ground. The bearded man let go the branding iron, pulled his own gun and motioned Lee to get down.

'Good work, Jeb,' he said. 'Reckon we'd better find out somethin' about this *hombre* before we take him back to the ranch. No doubt Bassard will make him talk then even if he won't tell us anythin'.'

'I can make him talk,' said the tall man, a vicious leer on his face. Lee glanced at him closely as he stepped close, saw the unmistakable signs on the other's features, the high-bridged, aquiline nose, the darkness about the complexion and the black eyes that watched him unwaveringly, pitilessly. There was something of the Apache or Comanche about this man, he thought, with a faint twinge of fear.

Coming right up to him, the other unbuckled Lee's gunbelt, but he did not let it fall to the ground. Instead, he kept a tight hold on it, running it through the fingers of his left hand almost caressingly. His lips were drawn into a hard, tight line, the tip of his tongue occasionally thrusting through them. Still smiling tightly, he walked around behind Lee. Devrin heard him moving around, but could not guess at what the man was doing. Then, without warning, the other's bunched fist, with the belt wrapped tightly around his knuckles, slammed into the small of his back, driving him forward so that his knees buckled and he almost collapsed on to his face.

Only by a tremendous effort of will was he able to remain upright, sucking air down into his heaving lungs, as darkness wavered in front of his eyes and a sharp-edged lance of pain forked through his body. Forcing himself erect, he waited for the other blows which he knew would surely come. He could make out the bearded man grinning savagely, but the other's face wavered and blurred in front of his vision and there was a dull throbbing pain at the back of his eyes, striking deep within his forehead.

His breath rasped in his throat, whistling between his tightly-clenched teeth. Behind him, the other grunted, then began to slam in a rapid succession of body blows, each one skilfully aimed at a particular part of his body, designed to give the maximum of pain for the minimum of effort on the other's part.

How long it went on for it was impossible for him to tell. When the punching finally stopped, he was swaying, almost unconscious, wanting to let the darkness reach in and overwhelm him so that there would be no more pain, yet somehow fighting against it. Once he was unconscious, there was no telling what they might do to him. Somehow, he had to stay on his feet.

The man moved around and stood in front of him. He said through his teeth: 'Don't you think you'd do better to talk? Who are you? What are you doin' here and why are you so all-fired anxious to meet up with Hague Bassard?'

'That's something between him and me,' Devrin said huskily, forcing evenness into his voice with an effort. He was swaying now, with his eyes half closed, scarcely seeing the other as more than a vague shadow. The hammer blows inside his skull threatened to tear his head asunder and he was acutely aware of the throbbing pain deep within his vitals.

A smashing blow on the side of the face jerked his head to one side. With an effort he succeeded in stilling the cry of agony that rose unbidden to his lips.

'I don't like jokes,' snarled the other.

Devrin shut his lips tight and said nothing. Muttering under his breath the other took a step forward. 'You still goin' to be stubborn?'

'I've got nothing to say to you.' Somehow, Lee forced the words through his bleeding lips. His tongue moved rustily between his teeth and the whole side of his face burned from the shuddering force of the blow.

'I know a dozen different ways that I ain't tried yet,' snarled the other.

'Don't you reckon we ought to get him to the ranch, just in case Monaghan or Bassard want to talk to him. If he's been beaten up too much he may not be in any condition to talk and they won't like that.'

'I said I can get him to talk,' snapped the other. He went livid, then stepped in and leaned forward, aiming a chop for Devrin's neck. He tried to roll his head to one side and ride with the force of the blow, but only partly succeeded. It was a hard, vicious chop. Vaguely, Devrin knew that a stab of agony, greater than anything he had ever known struck through him. Then the blessed blackness came and enveloped him utterly.

The man stood looking down at the fallen man in front of him, then drew back his foot and aimed a boot at Lee's ribs, but there was no response from the unconscious man. Turning, he snapped: 'Better get him into the wagon. I'll tie his hands and legs just in case he should come round on the way and try to make a break for it. We'll take his mount along with us. That looks like a fine piece of horseflesh.'

Together, they carried Devrin's limp form to the wagon and tossed it into the back. 'We'll finish this job and then head back to the ranch house,' said the tall man, scarcely moving his lips. His eyes were beady as he stared into the back of the wagon at Devrin's limp form. He dragged breath down into his lungs then moved back to the waiting steers, thrusting the cool branding iron into the glowing centre of the fire.

The enveloping blackness was too deep for Lee Devrin. Somehow, even though he tried his damnedest, it was impossible for him to force his way out of it. There was no top and no bottom. He sank for a limitless distance and then the motion reversed itself and he felt himself beginning to rise. The unconsciousness was all there was to him. Nothing else existed. Coming and going, as though it was somehow geared to the pulsing of his own heart, it stayed with him.

At length, after an indefinable time, he moved to the surface. There was a brief glimpse of reality. He was vaguely aware of movement and of light shining redly into his brain through the closed lids of his eyes. For a fraction of a second he opened them. The vicious glare forced him to screw them up tight in a sudden reflex gesture. Savagely, he hung on to the fleeting moment, strove desperately to stay above the surface even though it brought pain with it, not wanting to sink down into that fathomless darkness again; not knowing when, or if, he would come out of it again.

Gradually, he became aware of his position. He was lying on his side and when he tried to move his arms and legs, he found that he could not do so. Thongs dug deeply into his wrists and ankles and after a while he gave up the vain attempt and lay back, gasping for breath, but trying not to make any more noise than was necessary, not wanting any of the men to know that he was now conscious. From the jolting, swaying motion, he guessed that he was lying in the rear of the wagon he had seen. They were obviously taking him to the Double C ranch now that he had refused to talk back there. He lay quite still, listening to the creak of wood and leather, the dull muted talk from the two men on the wagon tongue. Their voices seemed to advance and recede in a curiously bewildering way and he could make out none of the words, nothing but a faint drone that gradually faded into a background noise which did not intrude on his consciousness unless he concentrated on it. His arms and legs throbbed agonisingly where the blood in his veins was dammed up by the tight thongs. Gritting his teeth, he tried to loosen them a little by wriggling his hands and legs around but they had been tied by a woodsman, someone who knew his business and it was impossible to loosen them even to the slightest degree.

There was a rising sensation of nausea in the bottom of his stomach where the kidney punch had thudded into his back, transmitting its agony all the way through his body. Working his tongue around his mouth he managed to make saliva and after a while, swallowing painfully, he found that his tongue was not as swollen as it had been earlier.

One of the men on the seat turned his head, saw Devrin's eyes open, said sharply to his companion: 'He's come round, Slim.'

The tall man looked over his shoulder, his gaze locking with Lee's. He nodded as though satisfied. 'We'll soon be there,' he said, then looked away again as though he had suddenly lost all interest in Devrin.

The wagon bucked and swayed from side to side as they hit a rough patch in the trail and every single movement sent pain jarring redly through Devrin's body. It must have been half an hour later as close as he was able to figure when he heard a hail from outside the wagon and a moment later, they drew up to a halt. The driver wrapped the reins around the upright, clambered down from the wagon. A moment later, the other man did likewise and Lee heard him moving around the side of the wagon. Then the back was lowered and he caught a glimpse of the tall man's face, peering in at him, a vicious grin fixed on his lips.

'All right, fella,' he said harshly, 'this is as far as you go.' He moved inside, squatted down beside Devrin and untied the thongs around his angles. 'On your feet.'

With an effort, Devrin lurched to his feet. There seemed to be scarcely any feeling left in his legs and the other thrust him roughly out of the wagon so that he stumbled forward on to his face in the dirt. A harsh laugh came from the small bunch of watching men.

'Ain't you goin' to untie his hands?' asked one of them, grinning hugely.

The other shook his head. 'I reckon I'll leave that to Monaghan.' Bending, he caught Lee by the arm, hauled him savagely upright and prodded him in the direction of the ranch twenty yards away. Blinking in the strong sunlight, Devrin tried to take in everything around him as he staggered forward, in spite of the throbbing ache at the back of his temples. He knew that he had been beaten up badly, that he had probably been kicked several tines while he had been unconscious. Every muscle and fibre in his body screamed silently with agony.

The tall man thrust the front door open, pushed him inside. Before closing the door behind them, he called over his shoulder to the men still in the yard. 'Get the wagon away and push his horse into the corral. I guess he won't be usin' it again.'

Desperately, Devrin fought down the rising sensation of nausea. The other forced him along the short passage, rapped on the door at the far end and waited for a reply from inside before opening the door and prodding him forward. Sucking in a deep gust of air, Devrin went into the room, with his captor crowding close behind him.

There was a man seated behind the table in one corner near the windows. He looked up as they entered, eyed

Devrin speculatively for a moment, then said sharply: 'I saw the wagon roll in, Slim. You're early. And who's this?'

'Fella tried to stick us up when we was brandin'. Guess he saw a little too much of our activities for his health.'

'So you brought him along here.' The other's brows went up slightly as he let his gaze rest on Devrin. 'He give you any trouble?'

'A mite, boss,' nodded the other. There was the faintest suspicion of a leer on his face. 'But we soon quietened him down.'

Monaghan, for already Lee had guessed that this was who the other was, said harshly: 'You know my orders, Slim. I don't want intruders snoopin' around the place. But you were ordered to see to it out there – not bring them back here.'

'I know, but I figured you might want to have a talk with this *hombre*, before we work out what to do with him. He said he had business with Bassard.'

Monaghan got to his feet, moved around the corner of the table, came up to Devrin. He said thinly: 'What do you want with Bassard?'

'That's entirely between him and me.' Lee said, facing up to the other. He saw the blow coming, but in his weakened condition he could do nothing to get out of the way of it in time. It struck him on the side of the head, setting his skull ringing again He bit his lower lip to prevent himself from crying out.

'I asked you a question, mister,' snapped the other tightly. 'I want an answer. And it had better be the truth, otherwise I'll turn you over to Slim here for half an hour. At the end of that time, you'll be telling me everything I want to know.'

Looking at the other's eyes, Lee did not doubt that he would do just that. He glanced around at Slim standing close to the door, a vaguely amused expression on his face.

73

'All right,' he muttered finally. 'I'll tell you why I want Bassard, but not in front of him.' He saw the other push himself off the wall, anger on his face, but even as Slim advanced on him, Monaghan said harshly.

'All right, Slim. Hold off.' Monaghan held up an arm. His gaze locked with Lee's for a long moment and there was a look on his face which the other could not quite fathom. 'I'll talk with this *hombre* alone.'

'But, boss. He may be—'

Wordlessly, the other went back to the table, opened a drawer and took out a heavy Army type revolver. Snapping open the breech, he loaded it from the drawer, then sat down and laid it carefully in front of him, within easy reach of his hand. 'I can handle him, Slim. Now get outside and wait until I call for you.'

The other hesitated, then reluctantly opened the door and stepped out, closing it behind him.

Lee said: 'Mind untying my wrists, Monaghan?'

The other smiled broadly, showing even white teeth. He shrugged. 'I figure I'd feel a mite safer if they were tied.' He nodded to the chair in front of the desk. 'But you can sit down if you wish.'

Gratefully, Lee lowered himself wearily into the chair. His wrists were chafed and raw from the leather thongs and he felt them burning every time he moved. The dull ache was still present in his belly but he forced himself to ignore it, concentrating on the other.

'Now, why are you here and what do you have to say to my foreman?' The rancher took out a slim black cheroot, lit it and leaned back, still keeping one hand on the table near the revolver, evidently determined to take no chances.

Devrin eyed him shrewdly. The other looked and sounded a hard man, but it was just possible that he might be a fair one. He felt a grim sense of amusement deep within him. Anyway, there was little he could do about it. If he tried to hold out on the other, he would be turned over to Slim and it was clear that the other knew enough Indian tricks to make a man talk.

'All right,' he said finally. 'Bassard has some information I want. Accordin' to what I've heard, he rode with Quantrill during the war and he was in the party that raided this part of the territory.'

Monaghan's eyes narrowed a little behind the blue haze of tobacco smoke. Finally he twisted a little in his chair. He said: 'I'm afraid I wouldn't know anythin' about that. I don't ask a man's pedigree when he comes to work for me. Just so long as he carries out orders and remains loyal. That's all I ask of anyone.' A pause, then: 'But what does this have to do with you?'

Grimly, the other said: 'I'm Lee Devrin. My family were murdered by Quantrill's men. They burned down the ranch and barn after killin' my folks. I got back from the north a couple of days ago, found out what had happened. If Bassard rode with Quantrill, then he's one of the men I want. And he can give me the names of the others.'

'And you expect me to turn Bassard over to you, just like that?' queried the other. 'He's a good foreman and whatever it was he did before he signed on my payroll means nothin' to me.'

'So what do you intend to do?' Lee asked pointedly.

The other smiled. 'Now that's a very interestin' question. You rode into one of my camps and saw quite a lot that you weren't supposed to see. Normally if that had happened, my men would have shot you down on the spot and buried you somewhere out there in the desert. But somehow, Slim figured you was a trifle different from any of the others who've butted into my affairs and he brought you back here. Not that it makes much difference anyway.'

'You don't intend that I should spread any of this

around,' Devrin said through his teeth.

'That's perfectly correct, Devrin. I can't afford to be generous. I've built up this spread from nothin'. I started off with a few head and now I have close on five thousand. Another ten years and I'll have all of the land you can see from the ranch and I don't mean to let anythin' stand in the way of that. A man's life means absolutely nothin' to me compared with that.'

In spite of the tight grip he had forced on himself, Lee felt the stab of fear pass through him, cursed himself inwardly for having been such a fool as to walk into this trap with his eyes wide open. He kept his face expressionless as he faced the other across the table. Monaghan isn't an animal, he thought fiercely, he can't smell fear. He can only see the outward signs of it if a man shows them.

Monaghan set his jaw, got to his feet and picked up the gun. Keeping a careful distance from Devrin, he went over to the door, opened it and called loudly: 'Slim!'

The tall thin-faced man stood in the open doorway within seconds of the other's shout. 'Yes, boss.'

'Take Devrin here to the barn and see that he doesn't get away. We have to play this deal carefully just in case anyone knows that he was headed this way.'

'Sure, boss.' The other nodded. Pulling the long-barrelled Colt from its holster, he motioned to Lee to precede him along the passage and out through the outer door.

'Into the barn – and hurry!' Slim said tautly. His gun gestured at Devrin.

Slowly, the other staggered across the courtyard towards the barn. Inside, it was cool, with the sweetish smell of hay in the air. There was an empty stall at the back of the barn and Devrin was forced into it. He saw the thick wooden stake driven deep into the floor, guessed that it was used for any high-spirited horses they might have. There was a

76

length of rope fastened securely to it with an iron ring at the end. A painful, but highly effective means of keeping an animal tied up.

'Sit down,' ordered Slim. He jabbed the barrel of the gun sharply into the small of Lee's back when the other hesitated. Sucking in a sharp breath, Devrin sank down on to the thin covering of straw, watched out of narrowed eyes as the other reached for the metal ring, forcing it open by bending the iron jaws on the floor, then snapping it shut on Lee's ankle. Stepping back, he surveyed his handiwork with a look of satisfaction on his smoothly dark features, then nodded.

'There now, I reckon that ought to hold you until the boss has made up his mind what to do with you. Not that your end is goin' to be pleasant. Far from it.'

Leaving this thought in Devrin's mind, he backed away, shut the door of the stall. Devrin sank back on to the straw, listened to the other's footsteps fade into the distance. A moment later, there was the dull hollow sound of the barn door being closed. Silence reached in all around him as he sat up and stared at his surroundings.

Monaghan turned the corner of the table in his room and then, acting on impulse went back and locked the door before sitting down, staring straight in front of him, his face worried. His fingers were interlaced in front of him, knuckles standing out whitely with the pressure he was exerting on them. The events of the past two days were something he had not anticipated. He might have known that some of the folk who had been killed here would have relatives who might come riding back, seeking vengeance once they discovered what had happened. Now that the time had actually come, he felt at a loss for something to do to extricate himself from this position into which he had been forced by circumstances.

He did not doubt that if this *hombre*, Devrin, got to Bassard as he had threatened, the other would talk and tell everything, implicating everybody who had been in that raiding party and was still alive. He could, of course, kill Devrin. Yet there were two things against this which he knew he would have to weigh very carefully in his mind before he did anything. Devrin was no fool and somebody, possibly the Danahers, were sheltering him. He recalled how Clem Danaher had been asking awkward questions around town the previous day and Bassard had agreed to see to it that he never made it back to his own place. Inwardly, he was not quite certain that Bassard had been successful in spite of what the foreman had told him last night. But there was that girl who could be just as stubborn as her father and she might cause trouble in town if he got rid of Devrin. In addition, Devrin would possibly be the first of several men riding back from the wars, men whose families and homes had been destroyed. They too would start asking around and he could not hope to silence them all.

Bassard was the weak link. Since he had first met the man in San Randido he had felt nothing but contempt for him; a contempt which had certainly been shared by Quantrill. The other had not trusted him and when they had ridden out that night to fire those farms and ranches, he had seen Bassard hiding back among the trees, not daring to fire a shot, not wishing to incriminate himself. Yes, there was no doubt he would squeal if Devrin began to apply the pressure to him.

Somehow, he would have to ensure that Bassard was permanently removed, but in such a way that it would divert suspicion from himself and on to Devrin . . .

# TRAIL BY GUNSMOKE

Monaghan's horse quickened its pace from a listless lope to a rapid gallop as he dug spurs cruelly into its hide. The midday sunblast burned down from the inverted furnace of the cloudless heavens, sending waves of heat and light shooting at him from all directions, dredging all of the moisture from his insides out through the pores of his flesh where the heat sucked it away thirstily.

Here, at the south-west corner of the Double C range, the lush grassland gave way to a stretch of eroded rocks of red sandstone and beyond that, there was the desert proper, rolling out to the distant horizon that shimmered in the heat haze. There was a creek a couple of miles ahead and this was his destination. Around the bend in the trail, where it cut out to the west and then swung back sharply on to the range, there was the line camp. Hague Bassard was there at that moment, would be leaving shortly before sundown to ride back into Fenton before heading up to the ranch house the next day.

Monaghan leaned forward in the saddle, narrowing his eyes to mere slits against the sunlight. In spite of the skin-blistering heat, his mood fitted the conditions. When he had left the ranch that morning, he had felt strangely restless and dissatisfied. Everything had seemed to be working against him. The sudden and unexpected appearance of this *hombre*, Devrin, had upset a lot of his plans.

Now, since he had been able to think things out, his scheming mind had given him the idea of getting rid of both these men in one blow. He left the trail and cut up into the gaunt rocks which probed like scarlet fingers at the heavens.

Reaching the creek, he stepped down and allowed the horse a chance to blow, as he bent at the edge of the water and splashed it into his face before drinking. He felt the sting of the icy water on his hands and face, reminding him of how hot it was. There was a cloud of buzzards wheeling high in the air over his head, circling in slow, lazy sweeps against the sky, like tattered pieces of black cloth. The scavengers knew that it was not safe for them to descend just yet though he was probably the only thing moving on the ground below.

Lifting his head, he slowly scrutinised the brush on the far bank of the creek where the ground began to rise steeply, forming a kind of headland thrusting out into the flat desert. He had little relish for the ride through that stretch of country, a green hell of chaparral and mesquite thickets, with patches of Spanish dagger and junco that could, together with the prickly pear, tear a horse's feet to pieces in a very short space of time. Had he plenty of time to lay his trap for Bassard, he would have ridden around it, even though that would have taken him out into the desert and added several miles to his trail. But he had very little time, he judged, glancing up at the westering sun. The sooner he got into position, waiting for Bassard to show up, the better. Whatever happened, he did not want to meet the other out here on the open trail.

Getting to his feet, he walked over to the horse, waited impatiently until it had finished drinking, then tightened the cinch where it had worn loose during the long ride out from the ranch. Swinging wearily into the saddle, he put the horse through the shallow water, and up the far bank. It shied a little as he moved it out into the fringe of jagged vegetation, but he held a tight, short rein on it so that even though it shook its head fiercely from side to side to indicate its unwillingness to move into the Spanish sword, it was forced to do so. This brush country formed a long, winding belt between the desert and the grassland. It was the home of hordes of vicious brown flies that attacked men and beast with a vengeful fury. Savagely, he swatted at them as they settled on him from all sides, biting and stinging every part of his exposed flesh with a merciless fury. The flies settled on the deep scratches in the horses's feet where the sharp-pointed leaves tore at its ankles.

He rode steadily through the spiny vegetation, knowing that it was hard on the horse, but that it was the only course open to him. At the further edge of the mesquite, he reined up and stared out across the more open ground ahead of him. Less than half a mile distant was the small clump of trees set on top of a low rise which was his destination. The trail ran some thirty yards to the left of them. Once among those trees, he could settle down and wait for Bassard, biding his time until the other, unsuspecting, was close enough for him to fire a killing shot.

Jerking up his head, he stared through the thick tangle of green that now lay all about them, closing in on the trail, narrowing it down until it became little more than a game run, dimly seen most of the time, winding and twisting through the mesquite. The sun continued to beat down mercilessly on him, burning on his back and shoulders. He thought of the creek they had just left behind, and wished that it might have been possible to hole up there and wait for Bassard to come. But this was a chore about which he could afford to take no chances.

Inside the trees, he made camp, staking out the horse in the small clearing out of sight of anyone riding the trail even in full daylight. He sat with his back against the trunk of one of the trees and smoked a cheroot, drawing the fragrant smoke deep into his lungs as he turned his plan over in his mind, making certain within himself that there was nothing he had overlooked, nothing that could go wrong at the last minute and bring everything to naught.

It seemed foolproof. With Bassard dead, shot in the back from cover, he would have rid himself of that danger which had been hanging like a sword of Damocles over his head since the end of the war and the law had turned its attention on the men who had ridden with William C. Quantrill.

He knew that he could trust Slim, back at the ranch to back him up in the rest of the plan. Make sure that Devrin escaped, but not to make it too easy for him to do so otherwise the other might become a little suspicious. He was banking on Devrin having spread the word around that he was trailing Bassard, that he wanted him to answer some questions. It would be easy then to get people to believe that Devrin had finally caught up with Bassard on this lonely stretch of trail, had gunned him down, dry-gulching him from the small grove, shooting him in the back before he had a chance to talk or defend himself.

Monaghan's lips curled into a satisfied grin as he mulled the idea over in his mind There were no flaws whatsoever in the plan, he finally decided. He would have killed two birds with one stone and he would make sure that it was all done perfectly legally. Devrin would be taken by the posse headed by the sheriff, brought back into town and tried before a jury. He himself, would see to it that the right men served on that jury and once they brought in their inevitable verdict of guilty, they would take Devrin out of town right away and string him up from the nearest tree.

He felt the sense of impatience riding him now, growing stronger within him with every succeeding second. It grew so intense that he found himself staring through the narrow gap between the trees where he could look out along the winding trail for almost a mile, willing the other to ride into sight so that he might watch him all the way until he drew level with his hiding place. But as yet, the trail remained empty, although in the west, stretching out along the entire horizon, the blues were fading swiftly and it was like looking on to the open mouth of hell, into some gigantic burning furnace, with the reds and raw golds billowing up from the grave of the sun, long orange fingers of flame poking around among the few clouds down on the skyline and some light purple starting to mix in with the other colours, showing that the twilight would be short and that night was already starting to move in.

There came the chattering, shrill wail of a coyote out on the desert somewhere. A little early, Monaghan thought with a fierce sense of impending fulfilment. The moon wouldn't rise for another couple of hours or so, giving him the goddess of the night at which to howl. He felt hungry to his heels, but he did not dare to light a fire and was content to sit back and chew reflectively on the strip of jerky from his saddlebag. It sated his hunger a little and he washed it down with cold water from his canteen.

A faint sense of unease began to work its way through him, rubbing the edges of his nerves raw, scraping them deeper than he had ever known before. Where the hell was Bassard? Why didn't he show up? If he had left the line camp when he should have done, he would have been in sight by now. In spite of the tight grip he had forced on his emotions, his fingers interlaced themselves in front of him, gripping together with a terrible strength. With a tremendous effort, he forced himself to relax. One by one, the minutes were chopping themselves off, each dragging itself past in a long tight agony of waiting. Patience was now not one of his virtues. In the old days, when he had been with Quantrill, he had known how to outstare a desert lizard until it had turned its beady eyes away from him and skittered off into the rocks. But no longer. The years had worn his patience thin, had tautened his nerves, pulling them like tight piano wires throughout his body.

God, where was he? The strain was starting to get at him. He thrust himself to his feet, picked up the long barrelled Winchester, checked that it was loaded with the catch off and moved to the very edge of the trees, kneeling on one knee, peering off into the growing dimness, listening with a part of his mind to the endless, eternal song of the wind sighing, moaning, shrieking and whispering through the swaying branches over his head.

Had something happened at the camp, making it necessary for Bassard to stay there for another night? Had the other finally decided that he no longer wished to be tied to a man who so obviously did not trust him? Monaghan knew quite well that Bassard was growing more and more suspicious of him, more wary, as the realisation grew in him that he was a constant source of danger, willingly or otherwise, to him.

He grew aware that he was fidgety, knew that it was bad to get this way. After all, he reminded himself, Bassard had no way of knowing that he was lying in wait for him here.

Squatting back on his heels, he dragged down a long breath, squinted into the fading sunglow. His muscles sagged, went limp for a moment and he wished that it was all over, that he could mount up and ride hell for leather out of there, back to the ranch, ready to pass the murder charge on to Devrin. That part would be easy, he thought. The other did not yet know what was in store for him, what plan had been built up against him. The release of tension lasted for only a brief moment. Then he pulled himself savagely together, gripped the stock of the rifle and forced himself to his feet.

Something was moving out there along the trail, a tiny black dot, made diminutive by distance but definitely growing larger as it came nearer. He sucked in a sharp gust of air, felt the cold perspiration break out on him once more as he narrowed down his eyelids and tried to make out the identity of the oncoming rider. He felt certain that it was Hague Bassard. It could be no one else. Yet there was always the chance that fate might play an unkind trick on him, that this might be some cowpoke riding the trail, heading for town, butting in on his play.

Crouching down, he waited. The man came on at an unhurried pace, taking his time. Evidently he did not intend to get anywhere before dark. The other was less than fifty yards away before Monaghan was sure. It was Bassard all right sitting tall and easy in the saddle, his face a pale grey blur in the dimness. The other turned his head slightly as he neared the clump of trees and seemed to be staring right through them, as if he could see Monaghan squatting there with the rifle trained on him, his finger bar-straight and tight on the trigger, just waiting for the right moment to fire.

A faint tingle went through Monaghan and for a moment he wanted to yell out aloud, do the honourable thing, warn the other that he was there, and give Bassard an even chance. But the impulse died almost as soon as it had been born. Monaghan had not got to be where he was without being utterly ruthless. It was a case of kill your enemy or be killed yourself. This was the maxim by which he fought and lived.

Squinting carefully along the barrel, he levelled the sights on the other's body, swinging the gun slowly as the man drew level, then began to move on, along the trail in the direction of the creek. He thought he heard Bassard whistling softly to himself, a lilting melody that sounded a little incongruous in the utter stillness of the early night.

The sound died suddenly, was swamped by the racketing din of the single rifle shot, the echoes bucketing back from the trees. Through the V of the foresight, he saw Bassard jerk and sway in the saddle, clutch at his chest, his body arching back over the cantle. Then, somehow, he came upright again with an effort, turning his head for an instant as though trying to catch a last glimpse of the man who had shot him down from ambush. Almost, he made it. Then a visible shudder passed through his body and he slipped sideways out of the saddle, hitting the ground with a thump, rolling a little way before lying still close to one of the upthrusting boulders. His horse, flinching away from him, lunged forward, then raced off into the darkness. Monaghan hesitated for a long moment, listening to the running horse in the distance, the abrasion of its hooves on the rocky trail fading swiftly into silence. It would not stop running until it reached the ranch, he thought to himself. Going back to the horse staked out in the clearing, he thrust the Winchester back into the scabbard, untied the horse, then led it down out of the trees and on to the trail. Bassard lay in a huddled heap near the rock and he approached the other slowly, sure in his own mind that he was dead, but strangely reluctant to go near him. Finally, he stood in front of the other staring down at the man's dull features. The eyes were open, wide, but seeing nothing, dull and washed clear of all expression. The lips were parted in a look of agonised, stunned surprise and a tiny trickle of blood had formed at the corner of his mouth, oozing slowly down his chin.

Satisfied, Monaghan swung up into the saddle, headed back in the direction of the creek. He could no longer hear the distant run of the riderless horse and touching spurs to his own mount, he swung off the trail, out towards the desert, not wishing to head through the chaparral and Spanish sword again.

For what seemed the hundredth time, Lee Devrin strained at the metal band around his ankle, struggling to loosen it a little, but it resisted all of his efforts and he knew that he was merely wasting his strength, that whoever had designed it, had intended it to hold a high-spirited horse, that there was no chance whatever of a man getting free of it unless he had some tool to saw through that band of tough metal.

He stared about him in the dimness, but there was nothing in sight that he could use and he sank weakly back on the straw, letting his thoughts run on in his head, striving desperately to think of some way out of this mess he had got himself into. It had been a fool's play on his part to ride alone into the Double C ranch and hope to get away with it. No man could brace this crew single-handed. Monaghan and Bassard must have prepared for any emergency with most of the smaller ranchers against them.

Hunger growled in his stomach, reminding him that he had received nothing to eat since he had been imprisoned there. Surely they would not starve him. He shook his head a little. Undoubtedly Monaghan had some plan to get rid of him, but it would not include starving him. He figured that he would get some food soon. Desperately he cast about him, seeking some means by which he could take advantage of this fact. If he could take the man who brought his food by surprise, he might be able to overpower him and

Wearily, he shook his head. He could no nothing, even if he did succeed in overpowering the other. Not with that band still clamped around his leg, fettering him to the ground. He digested this in his own way. On the face of things, there seemed little he could do. Maybe once they came and took him out, he might have a chance then to make his play.

He jerked his head towards the door of the barn as he heard a faint sound. A moment later, it rattled open and the dark silhouette of a man stood in the opening. The other came forward, walked towards the stall. Devrin saw his legs appear just below the half-door, then he pushed it open and stepped into the stall. There was a tray balanced in his right hand.

He watched Devrin warily out of the corner of his eye as he stepped forward, then set the tray down near Lee. 'Here's some grub for you,' he said harshly. 'Better eat it right now before it gets cold. Ain't no way of tellin' when you'll get another meal.'

'As bad as that?' Lee said tightly.

The man shrugged. He narrowed his gaze a little. 'Well, why ain't you eatin'?'

'Aren't you goin' to take this iron off my leg while I eat?' Devrin stared up at the other from the floor.

The other ran a cold glance over him, seemed to debate the proposition for a while, then shrugged. Digging into his shirt pocket he came up with the key to the iron loop, drew his Colt from its holster and laid it on Devrin with one hand while he twisted the key in the lock with the other.

'Guess it can't do any harm for a while, just so long as you're eatin',' he muttered. 'Though Monaghan says that you have to be kept locked up here all the time. But he's out ridin' at the moment so I guess he won't know anythin' about it.'

Devrin said nothing, but leaned forward, rubbing the flesh on his ankle where the sharp edge of the metal had cut deeply into it, abrading it raw and bleeding. His leg still felt numb from the tightness of it, as though it had dammed all of the blood in his leg, allowing none of it through his veins and into his leg. He felt a little of the feeling come back into his toes, although it brought with it a wave of tingling agony that was almost worse than the agony itself.

Sucking in his cheeks, he felt the ankle gingerly, but the hoop appeared to have done no permanent damage there.

'All right,' snapped the other. 'You've got it loose. Now better get that food eaten up. Hurry! I don't want any of the others comin' in and seein' you loose like this or it may get back to Monaghan and he's the devil incarnate when he hears that his orders have been disobeyed.'

'I can imagine that,' Devrin said dully. He pulled the tray towards him while the other stood with his back and shoulders against the wall, not once taking his eyes off him or lowering the gun in his hand. Evidently the man was taking no chances with him. The gun was held, ready cocked and he stayed at a safe distance while Devrin ate, chewing the food slowly, washing it down with the luke-warm coffee in the tin mug.

'You got any idea how long Monaghan is goin' to keep me here?' he asked at length, glancing up at the other's shadowy figure. Even as he spoke, he was judging the distance to the other, wondering if he would have any chance at all of reaching the man before he could pull the trigger and send a bullet speeding into his body. From that close range it would be virtually impossible for the other to miss.

The man uttered a sharp laugh, shrugged. 'I reckon he's already made up his mind what to do with you. Tomorrow at this time, I figure you'll be past carin' about it.'

'You goin' to be a party to murder?' Lee muttered, still keeping his gaze locked with the other's, disconcerting him.

The man looked away uncertainly, but his finger remained on the trigger. 'I reckon that if you come trespassin' on Monaghan's land, then you deserve all that you get.'

'And how are you figurin' on keepin' my death a secret. There are plenty of folk in the valley who know I was headed this way. When I don't get back they may start askin' awkward questions. Even if the sheriff in Fenton is in cahoots with Monaghan, he won't be able to stifle 'em all for long.'

The other grinned. 'You're underestimatin' the boss,' he said thinly. 'He's got everythin' figured out.' Rubbing his chin, he stepped forward a couple of paces. 'Guess I'd better get that leg iron back on you. Then you can sleep peaceful for the night.' There was a beat of sarcastic mockery in his tone. 'And don't try to make any funny moves. I get real nervous with this gun when I'm facin' a *hombre* such as you.'

Still gripping the gun in his right hand, he reached cautiously for the leg iron, closed his fingers around it and motioned with the gun. 'Stick your leg out this way, Devrin. Careful now, I don't want to have to shoot you, but if you make me I will. Even if it deprives Monaghan of his fun tomorrow.'

Resistance was useless. Slowly, feeling some of the strength come back into his limbs, Lee stretched out his leg across the straw, the other foot braced under him. As the man bent on one knee, he said quietly. 'Don't you figure you could lock me up by the other ankle. That one is pretty damned near rubbed to the bone?'

The other hesitated with the iron still in his hand, then shrugged his shoulders. 'Guess that won't make much difference. So long as Monaghan don't notice when he comes to take you out tomorrow.' His voice was thickened with malice.

Devrin drew back his leg, braced himself tautly. This was the only chance he would ever get. It had to be now or never. He uttered a low whistle through his teeth, saw the other jerk his head up at the sudden sound. For a split second, the man's attention was distracted from his legs. Savagely, giving the other no time to switch his gaze, he lashed out with his foot. For a moment he thought sickeningly that he had failed, that the other had been waiting for this move. Instinctively, the other leaned back, head jerking round, the gun in his hand swinging. Then Devrin's boot caught him on the wrist, knocking the gun from his grasp, sending it sailing into the far corner of the stall. With a shrill cry, the other staggered to his feet, swinging the heavy leg iron on the end of the short chain, using it as a weapon. Devrin ducked under it, felt the breath of air as the piece of metal missed his head by scant inches. Then his bunched fist connected with a satisfying solidity on the other's chin. The man reeled back, his shoulders hitting the wall behind him. His eyes glazed momentarily, but he was merely feinting. As Devrin stepped in, he side-stepped neatly, swung a haymaker all the way up from the floor. The impact of the blow plunged darkly all the way into his mind as he fell back. Seizing his advantage, the other lunged forward and it was here that he made his mistake, grew over confident, believing that he had Devrin at his mercy.

Shaking his head desperately in an effort to clear it, Devrin covered up rapidly, arms and elbows raised in front of his body, absorbing all of the punishment. Through a blood-tinged confusion, he saw the other still coming forward, his lips thinned back, showing his teeth in a savage grin. Devrin rolled and the Double C man smashed head first into the wall, yelled something harsh and guttural, turned instinctively, hurt but still on his feet, still full of fight.

This time, Devrin had the blood out of his eyes from the deep cut on his forehead and his mind was more or less clear. He met the other's charge with a right hand square on the nose, felt flesh and cartilage smash under his knuckles. His elbow came round with a neat precision, hitting the man's throat. Gasping hoarsely, struggling to drag air down into his lungs, his throat muscles heaving with the strain, the ranch hand fell back. His face was a mask of blood, his right eye puffed and closing rapidly.

Desperately, seeing that the fight was going against him, the other stumbled forward, threw his arms around Devrin's middle and fought to bear him backward with his weight, his hands laced together against the small of Lee's back, pulling tight with all the strength in his arms. Savagely, Devrin hammered blows at the other's face, short, chopping blows. But the other merely buried his face in Lee's chest and the blows lost most of their sting by the time they connected. Locked together, they fell back on to the straw as Devrin's spurs caught in a piece of wood on the floor. All of the wind seemed to have been knocked from his lungs as the man's weight fell on top of him, crushing down on his chest. In spite of the fall, the other still retained his hold around Devrin's middle and he bored down with his face, striving to snap his back. Devrin could feel the other's breath hot on his face as the man used all of his strength in an attempt to finish the fight there and then.

Somehow, he knew that he would have to break the other's grip soon or his spine would be snapped like a rotten twig. Bracing his right leg, he succeeded in getting it under him. Desperately, he heaved upward with all of his strength, throwing the other off as they rolled over on the floor. Taken by surprise, the other's grip slackened momentarily. The movement had renewed the throbbing in Lee's ankle, but he forced himself to ignore the pain as he broke free of the man's suffocating grip, threw himself back on his haunches, then smashed in two savage blows on the man's chin. A third chop just behind the ear was enough to finish it. The man's head lolled stupidly on one side and a long sigh came out of him. Swaying slightly, his head pounding with the strain, he struggled to his feet, stood staring down at the other for a long moment, then bent and unbuckled the other's gunbelt, buckling it around his own waist. Retrieving the gun from the corner of the stall, he checked it, then thrust it into the empty holster and made his way noiselessly for the door of the barn. It was almost completely dark now, with only a faint residual glow in the west by which to pick out details. A couple of yellow lights showed in the windows of the ranch house and as he stood there he saw three men walk over from the bunkhouse, angle around the corner of the building and go inside, closing the door behind them.

The corral was less than fifty yards away on the far side of the courtyard. Cautiously, he slipped out into the dimness, keeping to the shadows as far as possible, making his way over the dusty courtyard, his spurs raking up little eddies of dust, his feet making scarcely any sound at all. Two minutes later, he reached the wooden fence of the corral, paused there, peering into the darkness, searching for his own mount. He spotted it at last a short distance away and there were also a couple of saddles hanging on one of the wooden upright.

Taking one down, he climbed up on to the rail near the gate, whistled softly in the stillness. He saw his horse lift its head, gaze inquiringly in his direction, then give a faint whinny and move over to him. It had almost reached him when the door of the ranch house opened. Freezing into immobility, he crouched down behind the rail, knowing that if the man happened to look in his direction, he could not help but see him. The other came out on to the porch, stood for a second peering out into the night. There was the scrape of a match, a brief orange flare as the other cupped his hands to his face. In the light, Devrin made out the bearded features of one of the men who had brought him in that day. The other remained there for several minutes, smoking his cigarette. Devrin felt the sharp fangs of cramp begin to work their way through the muscles of his thighs as he crouched down, not daring to move his position by so much as an inch for fear of giving himself away. If he was discovered, he might be able to pick the other off, but there would be more men inside the house and across in the bunkhouse who would come running, and shooting, at the sound of gunfire. The odds against him getting away, even without a saddle, were slim indeed.

At last, when he thought he could hold the position no longer, the bearded man turned, dropped the stub of his cigarette into the dust of the courtyard, ground it out with his heel, then made his way over to the dark bunkhouse. Lee waited until he heard the door slam shut, then eased himself slowly to his feet, letting the breath gush from his lips in an audible sigh. It was the work of only a few moments to slap the saddle on to the horse, tighten the cinch, then move over and unlatch the gate of the corral.

Climbing into the saddle, he settled himself for a moment, still feeling the weariness in his body, the pain that spread like a dull ache through him from the beating he had taken. He hoped that he would be able to stay awake in the saddle long enough to put plenty of distance between this place and himself before that hired hand in the barn came around and gave the alarm.

He walked the horse out of the corral, across the courtyard and then up on to the trail that led towards the low hills to the north-east of the ranch. Behind him, there was no sound, nothing to indicate that his getaway had been noticed. But it was not until he was up in the lower ridges of the hills that he allowed himself to feel easier in his mind. He deliberately put the horse through some of the roughest country he could find so that they left no trail which could be followed. As yet he was undecided what to do. He could ride all the way into Fenton and report what had happened to the sheriff there. But unless he missed his guess, Monaghan was in good with the law and from what Clem Danaher had told him, he could expect no help from them. His only hope now would be to lie low for a couple of days – if he went back to the Danahers it could put them in danger and that was the last thing he wanted – and then he would make a further try for Bassard. But this time, he would make sure that he did not repeat his earlier mistake. He would find Bassard at his own time and at a place of his own choosing. Now that he knew just where he stood with Monaghan and the Double C crew, he would have a better idea of how to go about it.

Among the rocks, he allowed the horse to move at its own pace. His ankle pained him and there was a continual throbbing ache behind his eyes which refused to go away no matter how hard he tried to ignore it. The moon came up and by its light, he saw that the trail swung round, took a more south-westerly course. For a moment he deliberated dully on cutting away from it and continuing to the north, but knew that in his present condition he could not make good time off the trail and south-west seemed as good a direction as any.

They came to a sandy gully, rode along it slowly, the horse picking its way carefully among the shadows. For a time he gave some anxious attention to his back trail but after a couple of hours riding, with no sign at all of pursuit, he felt reasonably confident that he had been successful in throwing any of the Double C hirelings off his track.

At the end of the gully, it became clear of brush and in the cold eerie moonlight, he came out on to a low grassy rise dotted with scrub mesquite. Toiling to the crest, he paused for a breather, gazing about him. Nothing moved in all directions but in the tricky overtones of moonlight and darkness, the battalion of creeping shadows that flanked the trail endowed every bush and stunted tree with human form. During the daytime, it was a pleasant enough place considering the nature of the desert and the tangled thickets which lay to the north and west, but at night it seemed to come alive with faintly heard rustlings that spoke of tiny nocturnal creatures on their nightly errands of death and destruction. Straining to listen, cocking his head this way and that, Devrin sought to decide between fact and fancy. Mostly though, he knew only his tiredness, pain and hunger. The meal he had eaten back in the barn had been little enough and had not satisfied his all-consuming hunger. The night had become an endless nightmare of hunger and physical discomfort. He knuckled at his eyes where the white dust had clogged them, making them smarting and tender.

Strung-taut nerves and starvation were beginning to get the better of him, he thought weakly. But so long as he had his horse and the guns, he could make a fight of it if those men did succeed in tracking him down. He tried to put himself into Monaghan's mind. What would the other man do once he discovered that his prisoner had escaped? Certainly he would have to do something to stop him from talking. Already, he knew far too much for Monaghan to allow him to stay alive. And if that held true for Monaghan, it went double for Bassard. Once the other learned of his presence in the territory and his intentions, he would be on his guard, might even get some of the Double C men to follow him, hunt him down like an animal out here in this wild stretch of territory between the wide grasslands and the desert.

A sudden crash in the brush nearby brought him whirling round in the saddle, his hand reaching down for the Colt. It was half clear of leather when the buck leapt clear of the mesquite and dashed across an open stretch of ground, clearly visible in the flooding moonlight. Slowly, he let his breath out from between his tightly-clenched teeth, relaxed, lifted his hand to push back the brim of his hat. Most of the sounds he had heard during the past few minutes were satisfactorily accounted for. He backed the horse away from the rim, turned it with a sharp tug on the reins and rode at a steady lope through the tufted grass patches.

During the night, with the moon drifting slowly, majestically across the star-strewn heavens, he rode with pain and weariness, fighting down the agony that washed in waves through his leg. His lips too were bruised and felt as if they were swollen to twice their normal size and his tongue moved rustily around his teeth. The trail in front of him stretched out around the edge of the desert to the south, then on through a continuous thicket of mesquite and thorn, the horse pushing its way ahead now with a painful slowness, not liking this kind of terrain at all. The moon dropped to the west and slowly, the dawn began to brighten in the east at his back; at first only a faint diminution of the darkness, but then a perceptible flush of grey, turning slowly to a rose-coloured bar that hugged close to the horizon.

He moved downgrade for a little way where the trail wound tortuously through high-piled rocks. In the distance there was a round-topped rise covered with trees that now took on a distinct shape as the dawn brightened. He paused among the upthrusting boulders and forced himself to remember the terrain here. He must be somewhere very close to the southern perimeter of the Double

97

C range, he figured after a moment's reflection. He had circled around to the north then swung around west and south. Monaghan might have a line camp close to the perimeter wire, he guessed. From now on, he would have to keep his eyes open for trouble, although it was highly unlikely that, even if his escape had been discovered by now, word could have have got out as far as this.

Ten minutes later, they splashed across a narrow creek that rushed swiftly from the higher reaches, bubbling and churning over the rocky bottom. Reining up on the far bank, he peered closely at the dirt near the water's edge. There were the prints of horses there, he noticed, recent sign which had been made less than twelve hours before. Brows drawn closely together, his forehead wrinkled in thought, he glanced about him, more conscious now of danger than at any other time since he had ridden out of the Double C ranch.

Stillness lay around him, thick and tangible. His horse stood quite still, ears pricked up, but evidently sensing nothing out of the ordinary. With an effort, he shrugged the feeling away. He was beginning to get jumpy for no reason at all. That was a measure of his fear.

The prints in the soft, moist earth suggested that a man had ridden this way and then returned, but there had been another horse with him. Two distinct sets of prints were clearly visible in the mud. Slipping from the saddle, he bent and examined the marks more closely. Finally, he squatted back on his haunches and built himself a smoke while he thought things out in his mind. One of those horses had been riderless. He felt sure of that. The prints were not deep enough for it to have been carrying a man. Puzzled, he smoked the cigarette, all of his senses alert now, his weariness forgotten in the urgency of his situation.

Finishing the cigarette, he went back to the horse,

patted its neck as it lowered its head, then climbed back into the saddle. He rode on along the trail where it passed through thorn and mesquite, junco and Spanish sword, more worried now than before, anxious to scout the trail ahead of him now that it was getting light enough for him to see things clearly.

Crossing the tangled stretch of vegetation, he was inside the notch of a canyon before he picked out the faint murmur of riders somewhere in the distance. He lifted his head, tried to pick out the direction from which the drumming was coming, but hearing was deceptive in canyon-riddled country such as this where every tiny sound was channelled, and re-channelled and magnified out of all proportion.

The riders did not seem to be getting any nearer and at length he guessed that they were following a trail which ran almost parrallel to his and he dismissed them temporally from his mind. The horse jumped into a tired, dispirited run as he touched spurs to its flanks, its shoes striking a hard, metallic ring off the rocky underfoot.

Ahead of him, the canyon opened out a little as he saw that the tree-covered knoll which he had noticed from further back along the trail was now quite close, off to his right, holding a commanding position.

He glanced anxiously at the shadowed banks of rock on either side of him, eyes searching out any movement among the rugged boulders. The shadows were long and black up there, but empty as far as he could see. He turned a bend in the trail, then fought down the horse as it reared sharply and violently. In front of him, less than ten yards away, half-hidden in the shadows thrown by one of the tall columns of stone, the body of a man lay with arms and legs outflung, the ugly stain on his back just visible in the pale dawn-light.

# THE BIG FRAME

Dropping from the saddle, Devrin drew his sixgun, and advanced slowly on the other. The sprawled body made an incongruous sight, neat and smartly dressed, and only the stain in the cloth of his back and the small, ragged hole in material showing what had happened. Gently, he touched the other's wrist, feeling for the pulse, but there was no beat of life and judging from the stiffness of the limbs, the other had been dead for some hours.

So this was the reason for the prints he had seen back at the edge of the creek, he reflected. A man had ridden out seeking to ambush this man, had shot him down in cold blood and then ridden back, and the other horse had been the dead man's, riderless, heading back for home wherever that may have been. But why had he been killed like this? Certainly it could have been the work of one of the hotheads in the area. A frontier territory such as this was sure to have some men, quick to anger, needing no excuse to gun down someone in order to square a debt, real or imagined, a man without the guts to do it in the open, face to face.

Slowly, he worked the body free of the boulders, dragging the man backward on to the trail. The other's spurs carved thin grooves in the topsoil and he found himself sweating over the job. The dead man was no lightweight and the loose, upthrusting rocks made hard work of the task. He had lowered the body to the ground, was on the point of going back for his horse, intending to throw the other over the saddle and take him on into town when the swift run of horses sounded around the bend of the trail. Sound and riders came on at the same moment, the small bunch of men reining up ten yards away. In the faint light he caught a fragmentary glimpse of the star on the tall, moustached man's chest as his jacket flipped back. The sheriff swung himself down and came forward quickly, then swung on Devrin his gun out, covering the other. He said sharply: 'Shuck that gunbelt, mister.'

'Now hold on there,' Devrin said harshly. 'I've just ridden up and found this *hombre*. I was goin' to get him over the saddle and bring him into town.'

'So you say,' said the other ominously. 'Your name wouldn't be Lee Devrin, would it?'

'If you know that then I guess you know it is,' Devrin said tightly. His mind spun with the implications of this. The sheriff nodded his head slowly. 'I'm Sheriff Coulton,' he said, tight-lipped. 'We was tipped off that you were ridin' into this neck of the woods lookin' for Hague Bassard. Some feud you had with him.' He looked down at the dead man for a moment, then back to Devrin. 'Don't take much imagination on my part to see that you finally caught up with him.'

'You mean that this is Hague Bassard?' For a moment. Devrin felt a sudden chill in his chest. He stared down at the face of the dead man as if seeing it for the first time. The full realisation of his position came to him at that moment.

The man next to the sheriff uttered a harsh, derisive laugh. 'You tryin' to tell us that you didn't know, Devrin?'

'That's right. I'd no idea who the poor devil was. All I know is that I stumbled on him a couple of minutes ago,

101

just before you arrived on the scene. He was lyin' among those rocks yonder. If any of you care to take a closer look at him, you'll see that he's been dead for some hours already.'

'Don't need to look any closer,' said Coulton. 'I've seen all I need. Now drop that gunbelt, or I swear I'll put a bullet in you and save Fenton the time and expense of a trial.'

For a moment the temptation to reach for his gun was there, living briefly in Devrin's mind. Then he shifted his gaze slightly, saw the four rifles that were laid on him, the grim faces of the men behind them, and knew he did not have a chance in hell of outdrawing all of them. He would be dead before he could even drop one of them. Useless to try to resist. Slowly, he unbuckled the gunbelt, let it fall to the ground at his feet. He held the sheriff's gaze with his own, then said sourly: 'This is the sweetest frame I've ever seen, Coulton. You must be awful well in with Monaghan.'

'What do you mean by that?' snapped the other harshly. He took a step forward until he was standing directly in front of Devrin. 'You got somethin' to say, then say it out loud so that the rest of the men in this posse can hear it.'

'Sure.' Devrin felt the hot anger rising within him, was unable to force it down even though he knew that this was just what the other was wanting, was waiting for. 'You're in cahoots with Monaghan. He was the one who put this frame on me, although right now I'm not sure why he did it this way when he had me hog-tied back there in that barn of his.'

'You expect anybody to believe that,' snarled the Sheriff. He lifted his left hand and swung the punch all the way from his knees. In spite of his slight-looking build. there was plenty of strength in the other's wiry body and Devrin crashed back on to the hard ground, his head ringing from the savage force of the blow. It was the second time that night he had been hit, and hit hard. The blow rocked him, awoke all of the previous pain in his body. Weakly, he rolled over on the ground at Coulton's feet, expecting a kick and covering up instinctively against it, but it never came. The other stood back, breathing heavily, the barrel of the gun in his right hand lowered, his finger tight on the trigger. On his face was the tight expression of a man who was steeling himself to the point of killing a man. Then, slowly, he relaxed.

'Get on your feet, Devrin,' he said heavily. 'And another crack like that one and I'll drill you. Now get on to your horse and ride with us. I'm takin' you back into Fenton on a charge of murder. You'll find that we don't waste much precious time with two-bit killers around these parts. You'll get your trial tomorrow as soon as I can swear in a jury.'

Shakily, Devrin moved over to his horse, grasped the saddlehorn in his fingers and pulled himself up with a painful wrenching of arm and shoulder muscles. He winced as he touched his face where the other's fist had hit him. It felt as though his jaw were broken, but he guessed that it was just the numbing force of the blow which made it feel so swollen and useless.

'Two of you grab Hague's body and bring it in,' yelled Coulton. 'I figure he deserves a decent burial and we can show the townsfolk the sort of killer we've got here.'

Devrin shut his lips tight, watched dully as two of the posse got down, picked up Bassard's body and lifted it limply over one of their saddles. Then Coulton gave the order and they moved out of the canyon, through the thickets of thorn and mesquite. As he rode between two of the men, Devrin tried to think things out in his mind. He still failed to comprehend just what had happened, how everything fitted together, but he did not doubt that this was all part of the plan which Monaghan had built up

103

against him. The way he saw it – although it was extremely doubtful if he could ever prove it, if he would ever get a chance to prove it – was that Monaghan or one of his men had dry-gulched Bassard here and that his own escape from the barn had been deliberately engineered. Now that he came to look back on things quite objectively, he saw that his jailor had made it easy for him to get away, had apparently disobeyed orders by taking off that leg iron, giving him the one chance he needed to get away. Naturally, it had not been made too easy for him to make his getaway otherwise he would have become suspicious, and maybe got around to thinking things out more clearly. Instead, he had ridden blindly into this trap. Somehow, he had taken the trail which had led him to this spot. He saw now that it would not particularly have mattered if he had taken any other trail. The sheriff would have been warned by Monaghan and they would have picked him up sooner or later and pinned this murder on him.

His only hope now lay in Mary Danahar getting to hear of what had happened. Even then he failed to see just what she could do about it. Monaghan and the sheriff would have little difficulty in getting together a jury who would find him guilty on this charge no matter what evidence was offered at the trial.

The upgrade trail jerked him back in the saddle and he found it difficult to stay upright and the sun glaring in his eyes increased the sick feeling in his stomach. The ride back into Fenton took most of the morning and he was swaying in the saddle by the time they entered the main street and rode in a tight bunch in the direction of the jail. Reining up in front of the low-roofed wooden building, Coulton signalled him to get down, then dismounted himself.

'Get yourselves somethin' to drink boys on me,' called Coulton over his shoulder. 'I'll look after this coyote now.'

The men dispersed, heading for the saloon. Devrin heard them laughing and talking among themselves as they crossed the wide, dusty street. Then the barrel of the sheriff's gun prodded him painfully in the middle of the back, urging him up on to the boardwalk in front of the office. Coulton unlocked the door, nodded him forward.

'Inside,' he said tautly. 'And don't forget. I've got an itchy trigger finger and it won't take much, just the flicker of an eyelid for me to pull this trigger.'

'I guess that Monaghan must have you right under his thumb, Coulton,' Lee said harshly. 'If there's one thing I really despise, it's a crooked lawman.'

He half sensed the other's move a split second before the gun in Coulton's hand, swiftly reversed, came down on the side of his head. The blow was not hard enough to knock him out, but it pitched him sideways into the doorpost and he was forced to hang there while full consciousness returned.

'This is gettin' to be a habit with folks around here,' he managed to mumble through tightly-clenched teeth. Shaking his head to rid it of the ringing agony that pounded redly through his skull, he got to his feet. Out of the corner of his vision he saw Coulton standing there, the gun held steady in his hand, finger back on the trigger.

'I'm warnin' you, Devrin. More of that and you'll be yellin' for them to take you out and string you up.'

'You're just like the rest of 'em,' Devrin said softly. 'And I can guess how well Monaghan will have this trial rigged to ensure that the jury reach the right verdict.'

'Inside,' snarled the other viciously. He thrust Devrin forward, through the outer office and along the passage at the back, to where the four cells were situated. Unlocking one of the iron-grille doors, he motioned the other inside, slammed the door and locked it again, tucking the keys into his belt.

*

Lee sat on the edge of the metal bunk against the wall, rubbing the bruises on his chin, staring sightlessly in front of him at the hard-packed earth of the cell floor. He was able to think now. Before, things had been happening so fast that there had not been time to take them all in properly. At first, when those men had ridden up and the sheriff had ordered him to shuck his gunbelt, it had all seemed like a bad dream from which he would soon waken. But now it had become borne to him that this was no dream, that Monaghan had played his hand too well, had weaved this trap with a greater cunning than he had given him credit for, and it was because he had been so foolish as to underestimate the other so badly, that he would now pay for that folly with his life.

His brain still seemed a little numbed from the blows he had received, first from that ranch hand in the barn when he had broken free and then from the sheriff. Partly too, he felt numbed by the shock of his predicament. It was now only too clear how Monaghan and Coulton would be able to weave a watertight case against him. He had spoken out against Bassard, had been asking around town for him. Monaghan would testify that he had ridden out to the Double C ranch demanding to see him. They would soon pin down who he was, how his family had been killed and his home destroyed by Quantrill's men. From that point, it would be a relatively simple matter to establish that Bassard had been one of the men who had ridden with Quantrill, that it was logical to suppose that he had been wanting him to avenge his family.

Oh yes, it all fitted together so well that he felt sure that even an unbiased jury would have been forgiven if they had found him guilty in the light of all the circumstantial evidence which could be brought against him. Outside, he heard a vague muttering, realised that a small crowd must have gathered outside the sheriff's office. A faint smile of bitter amusement touched his lips as he listened to the ominous, threatening sound. By now, word would have been spread around the town. Many people would now know that Hague Bassard's body had been brought into town and that the man responsible for shooting him in the back was lying in jail awaiting trial.

He wondered briefly whether Monaghan would arrange for mob violence to take over control and a lynch mob to drag him from the jail, taking the law into their own hands. If he did this, it would mean that he was taking no chances on word getting out to any of the smaller ranchers, who may be persuaded by Mary Danaher, should she hear of what had happened, that he was innocent.

But almost as soon as the thought crossed his mind, he dismissed it. Monaghan would be very sure of himself now. He would want everybody in town to know that this was none of his doing. It would all fall on Coulton's shoulders as far as the townsfolk were concerned. The trial would be held if only to show that justice was being done.

Less than ten minutes before, Coulton had come to the door of the cell. There had been two other men with him and in their presence, Coulton had recited the charge against him in a monotone. The two men had nodded their heads in agreement, then left with the sheriff and he had been left alone to think things out. The case against him had been so built up that it was damning, virtually unshakable.

He rose heavily from the bunk, went over to the narrow, iron-barred window, gripping the bars with his hands as he peered through into the dusty alley. He had already tested the strength and firmness of the bars several times, knew them to be unshakable. There was no way out through the small window unless somebody hitched these bars to a horse and pulled them free from the stone of which this part of the building was constructed.

Rubbing his forehead in an attempt to get rid of the dull ache, he sat back on the bunk, tried to figure out how such a case could have been built against him. He had been over it again and again in his mind since he had been brought here and each time, the evidence seemed more conclusive. Now, it had reached the stage where he didn't want to have to think about it any more. All he wanted to do was get some food and lie down on the bunk and surrender his tired, bruised mind and body to sleep. Every nerve and fibre in him was screaming soundlessly for rest and he knew inwardly that he would have to get some before the next day, otherwise he would stand no chance at all. As it was, his chances of proving his innocence were so loaded against him as to be virtually non-existent.

Patting his pocket, he found that Coulton had left him his tobacco pouch and matches. At least, he could smoke. He built the brown-paper cigarette with slow, methodical movements of his hands. Finishing it, he placed it between his lips, lit it and drew the smoke deep into his lungs. His mouth and throat were so dry that he coughed as the smoke went down and his eyes streamed tears as he sat on the edge of the bunk.

Moving along to the door, he paused there, pressing his face close to the cold, unyielding metal of the bars, peering as far as he could along the narrow passage. There was the door at the far end leading into the outer office and he could just make out a narrow strip of light under it and hear the slow, measured tones of the sheriff, talking earnestly to someone.

Was it Monaghan in there, giving the sheriff his final orders, making certain that the lawman understood exactly what he had to do? It seemed highly probable.

Monaghan would have ridden hot-foot into town the minute he heard the news and knew that the first part of his plan had worked perfectly. Straining, he tried to pick out the other's tones, but muffled as they were by the thickness of the closed door, he could not be sure whether he recognised them or not.

Then he heard the corridor door open. Light spilled through into the passage and he caught a glimpse of Coulton's wiry figure outlined in the doorway before he stepped back into the cell, lowering himself on to the bunk, stretching himself out on it and feigning sleep. Footsteps sounded, coming closer, and there was the sharp jingle of keys. For a moment, a sharp thrill of apprehension went through him. Had they decided to take him out and kill him there and then, without going through the farce of a public trial?

The footsteps stopped outside the door. Keys rattled in the lock and he heard the door creak open. A moment later, a rough hand shook him on the shoulder, urging him to his feet.

'Wake up, Devrin. I've brought somebody to see you. Not that you deserve any help after the way you shot Bassard in the back. But the law demands that you should be represented at your trial unless you wish to defend yourself.'

Opening his eyes, Lee stared across the cell at the other man standing beside the sheriff. He was a short, stout man, wearing a black frock coat, a wide moustache giving him a genial appearance, but his geniality was belied by the ferret-like look about his eyes and the thin, high-bridged nose.

'Who's this?' Devrin asked harshly.

'This is Ben Shannon. He's a lawyer here in town. He's agreed to be your attorney at the trial tomorrow. My advice is accept his offer.'

Devrin grinned. 'Is this some trick thought up by Monaghan to make it all look real legal,' he said quietly, fixing his gaze on the lawyer.

'I'm not going to ask you a lot of silly questions, such as whether or not you did kill Bassard as they claim,' put in the other, as if he had not heard Devrin's words. He seated himself on the bunk, hands twisted together in his lap. Coulton stood near the door, the Colt in his hand, ready for trouble. He said sarcastically. 'Like I told you, Ben. He ain't the sort who appreciates anythin' that you try to do for him.'

'All I want you to do is leave me alone,' Devrin flared angrily. 'I know you for what you are, Coulton. You've got no more right to that sheriff's star you're wearin' than I have. You don't uphold the law around here. Monaghan is the law, the only law, and you know it.'

Shannon said quietly. 'I'm afraid that making these statements against the sheriff won't help you at all, Mister Devrin. I hope that you understand the seriousness of the charge against you.'

'I understand only too well how Monaghan has rigged the evidence to frame me with this murder charge,' Lee said positively. 'If you want to help me, then get word of what has happened to Mary Danahar. Let her tell you of what happened to her father, how Bassard and Monaghan bushwhacked him along the trail, left him for dead.'

Out of the corner of his eye he saw the gust of expression that flashed over the sheriff's face, a look which was quickly hidden as the other saw him turn his head. But Devrin had seen enough. He went on quickly. 'Sure, that's right, Coulton. Monaghan slipped up that time. Clem Danaher wasn't killed as he figured. He's still very much alive and now that I think of it, maybe it was Monaghan who fired the shot that was intended to kill Danaher and he got afraid that maybe Bassard would spill what happened to someone else. So he cleverly arranged for Bassard to be killed, maybe did it himself, because he wasn't at his ranch yesterday. Then it was easy for him to frame me for the killin'.'

'All of this is just the sort of wild talk that we expected from you,' broke in Coulton. He took a step forward, bringing up the barrel of the gun as he did so, then lowered it as he caught Shannon's look.

'I agree with you, sheriff, that we should not attach too much importance to this statement. Bassard was, as we all know, Monaghan's foreman. They had been close friends for many years. So there was no reason whatever for Monaghan to want to kill Bassard.' He turned his gaze on Devrin. 'Whereas we have plenty of evidence to suggest that you wanted to destroy Bassard ever since you discovered he was one of the men who rode with Quantrill when they raided this part of the frontier durin' the war.'

Devrin smiled thinly. 'Seems to me that for a lawyer who is supposed to be defendin' me for murder, you're pretty biased already, you've either made up your mind that I'm guilty, or it's been made up for you. Either way, I don't need your services. I'll act as my own defending attorney tomorrow.'

Shannon stiffened. Then he got abruptly to his feet, stared down with cold eyes at Devrin. 'Very well, if that's the way you feel about it, I'll withdraw my offer.' He moved towards the door. 'Let's get out of here, sheriff. The sooner they hang this killer, the better I'll like it.'

There was a wide, mirthless grin on the sheriff's face as he opened the door, stepped out close on the heels of the other, locking the door behind him. For a moment, he remained there in the passage, peering in through the bars. Then he moved off after Shannon. The door at the far end of the passage closed with a hollow sound and there was silence again.

Sinking down on to the bunk, Devrin found himself trembling a little, from suppressed anger and apprehension. It seemed clear now that they did intend to go through with this trial – and just as surely, they meant to find him guilty of murder and hang him immediately afterward.

He stretched himself out on the bunk, staring up at the dark ceiling of the cell over his head. The minutes passed slowly. The hunger inside his belly increased its gnawing at his vitals and the cigarette had done nothing to ease it. How long he lay there before he heard the distant door open, it was impossible for him to tell. When Coulton appeared at the door he did not move, but lay listlessly on the bunk, not bothering to turn his head. Thrusting the tray between the bars, Coulton said harshly.

'Somethin' for you to eat, Devrm. We don't want you faintin' at the trial tomorrow.'

Swinging his legs to the earthen floor, he got to his feet, picked up the tray and carried it back to the bunk. Coulton stayed where he was just outside the cell, watching him closely.

Chewing slowly on the food, Devrin said: 'You reckon I'm guilty of this murder, Coulton?'

The other looking at him sharply, said: 'Reckon that ain't for me to say, Devrin. A jury'll decide that after they've heard all the evidence.'

'All the evidence?' The other laughed mirthlessly. 'You want to know what the truth really is?'

Coulton seemed on the point of saying something, then bit it back, changed his mind, said tersely: 'If you figure it's goin' to help you to tell me your version, then go ahead. It's no skin off my nose to stand here and listen to you. I've got to stay here in the office all night anyway, just in case any of the hotheads in town get it into their minds to come over here and take the law into their own hands.'

'Wouldn't think that would bother you over much.' Devrin spooned the warm broth into his mouth, mopped it up with the bread. 'At least it'd save you the trouble of gettin' me into court and then hangin' me. And all the time, you'd be plagued by the thought that maybe I am innocent, that you've strung up the wrong man.'

Coulton shook his head, with a faint smile on his thin lips. 'I won't lose any sleep over that, Devrin. As far as I'm concerned this is an open and shut case. If I ever saw a guilty man, then you're it.'

'If you'd checked Bassard's body like I told you to, you'd have satisfied yourself that he'd been dead for some hours, long before I stumbled on him.'

'How do I know that you didn't kill him, then go back for somethin'. Maybe to see if he'd been found?' queried the other.

'Because all day yesterday I was held prisoner at the Double C ranch. I went there to try to find Bassard, that much I'll admit. But he wasn't there and Monaghan seemed convinced that I'd seen too much for my health. He intended killing me but makin' it look like an accident. Then I figure he got to thinkin' about Bassard and decided he could kill two birds with one bullet. So he set things up to make it look as though I'd found Bassard and shot him in the back. Trouble is that when I found Bassard, there were questions I wanted to ask him, important questions.'

'Such as?'

'Such as the names of those other men who rode with Quantrill that night my family were murdered and the ranch burned to the ground. Bassard was only one man, and probably one who had little to do with their deaths. It was the others I wanted named and it isn't likely I'd shoot him in the back. I'd have questioned him first and then if it had come to a gunfight, I'd have killed him after givin' him an even chance.'

'We've only got your word for any of this,' said the other heavily. 'And I can guess who the jury is goin' to believe.' His smile widened. 'Mister Bassard was well liked in town and Monaghan is a very important man.'

'That doesn't put him above murder,' Devrin said harshly. He laid the empty tray down on the floor at his feet, watched the other narrowly from beneath lowered lids. As he had hoped, Coulton opened the door and stepped inside to pick up the tray. Waiting until the other was close to him, bending forward, the gun still held in his right hand, but the barrel pointed towards the floor for the second that he leaned forward for the tray, Devrin launched himself forward, thrusting away from the bunk with all the strength in his legs. His outstretched fingers clawed for the sheriff's gunhand, reaching for the gun.

Almost, his fingers closed about it. Then the sheriff swung back, arm going behind him for a moment. There was a faint leer on his face which told Devrin that he had been expecting this move, had been waiting for him. As the other stepped back sharply, Devrin over-reached himself, stumbled forward on the uneven floor. Unable to help himself, knowing that the descending butt of the Colt in the lawman's hand was arcing down on his unprotected head, he tried to roll away from the blow, but only partly succeeded. The gun butt struck him savagely on the side of the skull. There was a crash like thunder that roared all the way through his brain. Then he was falling forward and he kept on falling even after his body hit the floor, down, down into a deep and fathomless darkness with no bottom, an all-enveloping blackness that swallowed him completely.

When he eventually came round, he was lying on the bunk

inside the cell and there were the first faint red rays of the rising sun streaming in through the narrow window. Weakly, he sat up, but was forced to let his head fall back again as pain jarred through his skull. He felt spent and dizzy and there was dried blood encrusted on the side of his head just above his ear. He touched the spot gingerly with his fingertips, winced as agony lanced into his head. Drawing in a deep breath, he propped himself up on to his elbows, forced himself to keep his eyes open in spite of the pain and the throbbing of his own blood in his ears. He tried to remember what had happened, but memory returned only slowly and he was still struggling to recall the events of the previous evening when he heard Coulton coming along the corridor, stopping outside the door.

'I hope you're goin' to behave yourself a little better this mornin',' said the other meaningly. 'The next time you try a trick like that I'll let you have it.'

He pushed the breakfast tray into the cell. 'Here's a bite to eat. Better hurry. The court convenes in half an hour and I want to get you there in one piece. There are still a handful of men in town who'd prefer to string you up without a trial, if they get the chance. I've got some of my men out front watchin' for 'em.'

'You make it sound as though everythin' is goin' to be done real nice and legal so that you can come back here when it's all over with a clear conscience and take the blood money from Monaghan without any trouble.'

'Stop that kind of talk,' snapped the other. 'If you want that breakfast then go ahead and eat it.'

For a moment, rebellion urged him to pick up the tray and throw it in the other's face, but he fought down the feeling, picked up the tray and began to eat. There was still the chance that word might reach the Danahers in time for them to take a hand in these proceedings, although at the moment he could not see what the girl could do to help him unaided.

Coulton took the tray away when he had finished, came back twenty minutes later, opened the door and stood on one side, motioning him out into the passage. 'Don't try anythin' here,' he warned ominously. 'I've got men in the outer office and along the street. They have orders to shoot to kill if you try to make a run for it.'

Devrin shrugged. Better to bide his time than risk almost certain death in the street. The sun was higher than he had thought when he stepped out of the office, on to the slatted boardwalk. A small crowd of people had gathered outside the building and he saw their hostile eyes fixed on him as he made his way along the dusty street, flanked by two of the possemen, with Sheriff Coulton bringing up the rear.

The courthouse was set a little way back from the main street, with the bank on one side of it and a large grain store on the other. More townsfolk were standing outside the building as they approached and Devrin heard the faint muttering as he pushed his way through them.

'Why don't you lynch the killer now and be done with it, Sheriff?' yelled one of the watching men hoarsely.

'I'll get a riata,' said another in the front rank of the onlookers. He made to move away, but Coulton stopped him. 'Hold it right there, Charley. There'll be no lynchin' while I'm sheriff of Fenton. We're aimin' to try this *hombre* for murder and a jury will decide whether he's guilty or not. If he is, then we'll have him strung up by noon.'

'Reckon they'd better find him guilty then, Sheriff,' said the other tautly. 'Otherwise we're likely to make our own law right here. No killer is goin' to go free in Fenton, specially one who shoots men in the back.'

The muttering broke out afresh in the crowd and the two possemen pushed Devrin inside the building as though anxious to avoid any trouble, realising that if the crowd took matters into their own hands, they were hopelessly outnumbered.

The judge was a fat, cheroot-smoking individual who rapped loudly for silence as Devrin was shown into the enclosed section close to the jury. He turned his attention to the men seated on the two benches set against the wall. One glance was enough to tell him that each had been hand-picked, that as he had suspected, the jury was rigged. Looking around the small courtroom he tried to pick out anyone he knew but there was no one.

'This court will come to order,' said Judge Hendry loudly. 'You all know why we're here. Sheriff Coulton. I want you to tell the jury what happened yesterday.'

Coulton got heavily to his feet, striving to look important. He gave the judge a stare, took time to suck through his teeth, then began: 'I got word yesterday afternoon that someone had been in town askin' around for Hague Bassard.' He grinned. 'Naturally, I figured that it was of no account and that Bassard could take care of himself if there was any trouble. I figured that it was maybe one of the nesters out for blood as before. Ain't the first time it's happened whenever one of 'em has got a little drunk. Then Mister Monaghan rode in and told me he was worried about Hague, said he was supposed to have left the line camp some time durin' the mornin' but that he hadn't got back to the ranch and he wasn't nowhere in town. He asked me if I'd take out a posse and have a look around along the trail.'

So it had been Monaghan who had passed the word to the sheriff about Bassard, Devrin thought tightly. That could mean only one thing. It proved that Monaghan had been responsible for Bassard's death, even if he had not been the man who had actually pulled the trigger. But that was not going to be an easy thing to prove. In fact, it would be damned near impossible, because if he knew

Monaghan at all, the other would have cleared his trail behind him, leaving nothing whatever to chance.

Coulton went on slowly, pompously. 'I took out a posse and we rode along the trail that Bassard would have used. It was a little after sun-up that we came on this hombre here, kneeling beside Bassard's body. Hague had been shot in the back while he'd been ridin' past a clump of trees. We reckoned that Devrin had hidden there and killed him just as he rode past. Hague never had a chance.'

'So you brought him back here for trial together with Hague's body,' commented the judge.

The sheriff nodded. As he sat down, there was a sudden movement at the back of the courtroom. Devrin glanced round and saw that Monaghan had come into the room, seating himself at the back. The judge who saw him at once, said almost fawningly.

'I see that Mister Monaghan has arrived. Would you come up and tell the jury what happened.'

Monaghan rose slowly, deliberately to his feet, came forward. 'This man rode up to my place asking for Hague,' he said in a low, measured tone. 'When I asked why he wanted him, he refused to say, claimin' that it was something between Hague and himself, no business of mine. I told him that Hague was my foreman and he was out at the line camp, but he'd be leaving it within a few hours and headin' back to the ranch.'

'Did you tell him which trail Hague would be using?' asked the judge, leaning forward.

'I may have mentioned it,' said the other. 'Come to think of it, I'm sure I did, just before he rode out. I reckon he took that trail too when he left the ranch.'

'That is a damned lie and you know it,' Devrin said loudly, getting to his feet. He faced the rancher across the courtroom. 'You had me kept a prisoner in that barn of

118

yours until I succeeded in gettin' away just before night-fall. And I was still there, shackled to a post in the rear stall when Bassard was shot in the back.'

Judge Hendry banged loudly on the desk in front of him. 'The prisoner will remain silent until he is given his chance to speak,' he said forcibly. 'I will not tolerate these outbursts in my court.'

Turning to Monaghan, he said more calmly. 'Did you see anythin' of Hague until you saw him in the mortuary here in town?'

'No.' Monaghan's voice was a melodramatic whisper. Lifting his head, he glared across at Devrin. 'I see now that I should have taken this man's threats seriously, maybe sent out some men to warn Hague. But at the time I never thought he intended to kill him.'

'I think we can all understand that, Mister Monaghan,' said the judge quietly. 'Now unless there are any questions the jury would like to ask, I don't think we need trouble you further.'

Sitting beside the two armed possemen, Devrin listened to the damning evidence which was made out against him with a web of lies and half-truths. Evidently Monaghan had briefed these men well. They made everything sound so utterly convincing that by the time he stood up to speak in his own defence, it was obvious that he would not be believed.

After he had finished his story, Judge Hendry said slowly: 'You claim then that you were kept prisoner by Monaghan because you came across some of his men branding steers they had rustled and that while he was away from the ranch, as you claim shooting his foreman, you were allowed to escape in order for this shooting to be pinned on you.'

'Evidently neither you or the townsfolk here believe that Monaghan is capable of that,' Devrin said bitterly.

Judge Hendry was quite composed, although there was a faint flush staining his face. 'What we think of Mister Monaghan is quite beside the point here,' he said thinly. 'The point at issue is the death of Hague Bassard. Frankly, I can see no motive for Monaghan wanting to shoot his own foreman, and here in town it has been common knowledge that they were the best of friends. On the other hand, you came here with the vowed intention of meeting Bassard, forcing him to tell you the names of other men who rode with him during the war, implying thereby that you then intended to kill each and every one of those men out of a spirit of revenge for what they did. Whether or not you believe that you had that right does not alter the fact that Hague Bassard was shot in the back without being given a chance to defend himself and that makes it a charge of murder.'

'You know damned well that Monaghan is at the back of this. Whether he looks it or not he's the biggest man around here, he owns the most cattle and he has the most money. And that makes him the most important man in Fenton. It means that he has only to give an order and everybody jumps to obey it, otherwise they will undoubtedly regret it.'

The other was still controlled. 'Are you implying that Monaghan controls the law here?'

'I've met up with this kind of set-up before,' Devrin said acidly. 'It won't be the first time or the first place where it has happened. I don't need to look at those men sittin' there on the jury to know that their minds were made up long before they came into this courtroom and I know who made their minds up for them.'

There was a rising murmur from the crowd at the back of the room. Judge Hendry waited until everything was quiet again, then he said firmly: 'I reckon you've said all you intend to say in your own defence. We've heard your version of what happened and we've heard the evidence of all the other men concerned. The jury will now retire and bring in their verdict.'

Out of the corner of his eye, Devrin saw the men on the benches conferring among themselves in low voices. Then the tall, hatchet-faced man at the end of the bench got to his feet, gripping the low rail in front of him.

'I reckon we don't need any time to do any considerin', Judge,' he said loudly. 'We all figure that he's guilty of murder.'

The judge nodded his head slowly, evidently satisfied by the verdict. From the edge of his vision Devrin saw the faint smile of triumph on Monaghan's face as the rancher leaned back in his chair. Everything had worked out just as the other had planned. From the rear of the courtroom, a man shouted. 'I'll go get a rope and we'll string him up right now.'

# QUICK JUSTICE!

Devrin knew himself to be in great danger. There was no way of getting out of the courtroom. Already, the two possemen had moved closer, hemming him in, hustling him towards the door leading into the street. The crowd which had thronged the benches at the rear of the room had dispersed rapidly as soon as the verdict and sentence had been announced,

Before he reached the door, Monaghan came forward, lips parted in a faint smile. He said harshly, 'I warned you about this when you rode up to the ranch, Devrin, but you didn't take any heed. Now you have only yourself to blame for what has happened.' He turned to one of the possemen. 'I reckon you'd better tie his hands behind his back, Hank. Just in case he should decide to make a try to get away.'

Devrin was forced to stand still while his wrists were lashed tightly behind his back.

Stepping forward, Coulton glanced at him, then across at Monaghan. He said quietly, 'You don't need to witness this hangin' if you don't wish to, Mister Monaghan. I'll see that the sentence is carried out.'

'I'll come along,' Monaghan said softly. 'I want to make sure the the coyote who shot Hague in the back gets all he deserves.'

'Someday,' Devrin said thinly, 'that wish way come true. Maybe far sooner than you figure.'

'Just what do you mean by that?' snapped Coulton.

'I'd have to draw you a picture to make it any plainer.' Devrin said as he was forced out through the door and down into the street. The crowd parted as Coulton and the two possemen forced a way through.

With an effort, Coulton kept his voice under tight control as he said: 'Could be I'm a little dumb, but you'll have to spell it out for me.'

'All right. Most of you know deep down that I'm not the man who shot Bassard. Monaghan here did it, but there ain't no way of provin' it. Not to your satisfaction anyway. That's why that jury back there was carefully picked so they wouldn't even have to retire to find the right verdict.'

'Get moving, Devrin,' snapped Coulton. 'We don't have all day to finish this.'

One of the men had taken a lariat from his saddlehorn and moving ahead of the crowd reached the trail where it led out of town. Tossing one end of the rope over an out-thrusting branch of the lone sycamore that grew beside the trail, he let the noose hang loosely, waiting for the others to catch up.

'Bring a horse somebody,' yelled Monaghan.

The crowd parted as the black-bearded man Devrin had met up with at the Double C ranch came forward, leading a chestnut mare. 'Ain't no saddle on her,' he said, grinning broadly. 'But I figure that won't matter for all the time he'll be needin' her.'

Sheriff Coulton stood in front of Devrin and looked him steadily in the eyes. 'This is the first time I've done this since I've been sheriff of Fenton,' he said harshly. 'But I knew Hague Bassard well and I figure you're deservin' of this. Maybe it'll make any other coyotes like you think twice about ridin' into Fenton and bushwhacking honest men.'

He settled the noose around Devrin's neck, then motioned to a couple of men who came forward and hoisted him into the saddle. Three other men moved around to the other side of the tree, caught hold of the free end of the rope and hauled on it with all of their strength, tautening it so that the noose constricted Lee's neck, choking him, shutting off the air in his lungs.

Hoarsely, he said: 'I didn't kill Hague Bassard, Coulton. Maybe one day you'll find that out for yourself and realise that you hung an innocent man.'

'Stop lyin',' muttered the other. He gave Devrin a sharp, feral stare. 'You're as guilty as any killer I've ever seen. You wouldn't be like them if you didn't say you were innocent now that you see hell starin' you in the face.'

He stepped back towards the crowd, stood beside Monaghan, then gave a sharp signal with his right hand. The three men pulled more heavily on the rope, half hoisting Devrin off the mare's back. He felt the rope tighten agonisingly around his neck, felt the dull thunder of blood pounding through his forehead, drumming incessantly in his ears. His breathing was shut off. Brilliant lights of all colours flashed across his vision and there seemed to be a band of darkness hovering tantalisingly just at the edge of his vision where he could not make it out clearly. Involuntarily, without any conscious feeling, his legs began to kick and struggle. He knew that it would be only a moment or so before the man standing close to the mare gave the animal a sharp slap on the rump, sending it plunging forward, leaving him kicking for one brief instant in the air, before the downward jerk of his body sent him dropping out of that world and into eternity.

The man behind the horse lifted his gloved hand, turned his head to glance at Coulton, ready to slam his palm down on to the horse's hide. But the move was never made. There was a sudden, unexpected roar that hammered painfully at his ears, cutting through the thunder of pounding blood. The next second the pull of the rope slackened and he was just able to suck air down into his heaving lungs. Through blurred vision, he stared about him, realising dimly that the rope lay on his shoulder, and for one wild moment he thought that the sheriff had had a change of heart and had cut it through. Then he saw the slim figure that stood among the boulders on the far side of the trail less than ten yards away.

The tears in his eyes threatened to blind him as he tried to make out who it was. Even when his vision cleared and he recognised the other, it was still difficult to believe what he saw.

'You – Coulton, cut those ropes around his wrists,' called Mary Danaher in a clear, ringing tone. 'And don't forget, the first wrong move you make, there will be a bullet in you and the next will be for Monaghan.' There was no mistaking the menace and grim determination in her voice.

Edging forward, the sheriff reached up and sliced through the ropes which bound Devrin's wrists. With an effort, the other pulled the noose away from around his neck, hurling it away from him as if it had been a rattler he was holding. His throat was sore and bruised and his lungs seemed unable to get as much oxygen from the air he drew down into them as they needed. But his head was clearing rapidly and he gigged the mare slowly forward until he was alongside the girl.

'Are you all right, Lee?' she asked anxiously.

'I am now,' he said, reassuring her. 'But it was a damned close thing. Another second and you would have been too late.'

She nodded slowly. Sweeping her glance over the assembled men, she said very softly, 'I'm going to give you exactly ten seconds to get out of here. Any of you still here after that time will get all that's coming to him.'

'You can't get away with this,' stormed Coulton. 'You're helpin' a convicted murderer to escape.'

'You think I care for the kind of justice that you mete out here in Fenton,' said the girl, her tone dripping with sarcasm. 'I've learned enough of that to know how your courts work. Monaghan gives the orders and you and your picked jury carry them out.'

'This man shot Hague Bassard in the back,' said the Sheriff, fighting to control his voice. 'He was found guilty on the evidence. There was no other verdict that could be reached.'

The girl shrugged her slim shoulders. 'Personally I know he didn't shoot Bassard in the back. Not that he didn't deserve it. Now move – everyone of you.'

The threat in her voice was enough. Not until they had gone did she relax a little, and then only to motion towards the rocks. 'My horse is back there,' she said quickly. 'We must get away from here quickly, before they pluck up enough courage to come back.'

Turning, he moved quickly into the rocks, to where her horse stood patiently. Swinging lithely into the saddle, she thrust the rifle into the scabbard, rode down on to the trail.

'Where did you learn to shoot like that?' he asked, as they rode swiftly along the upgrade.

The girl smiled. 'I had to learn how to use a rifle by the time I was fifteen,' she said, noticing the look of amazement on his face. 'Times were hard here during the first year of the war. Most of the men were away fighting and we were forced to fend for ourselves. We often lived on what we could shoot and when you're starving, you soon learn how to hit a quail at two hundred yards.'

'I'm mighty glad that you happened along when you did,' he said fervently. 'Those *hombres* sure meant to finish me back there.'

'It was no mere chance I happened to be there,' said the girl, glancing at him out of the corner of her eye. 'We heard from the neighbours that you had been brought into town by the Sheriff and his possee and that they were holding you in jail for killing Bassard. At first I thought that maybe you'd found him in one of the saloons and fought him fair, but then they told us that the story was you'd shot him in the back somewhere along the trail.'

'And you believed that?'

The girl shook her head emphatically. 'I knew that you had every cause to hate Bassard and that you would kill him, but only in fair fight. It wasn't in you to shoot a man down from ambush.'

'I'm glad,' Devrin said quietly. They rode out on to the top of a rocky rise from where they could look back along the trail towards the town. A few moments later, they spotted the cloud of dust far off along the trail, knew that Monaghan did not intend that he should get away as easily as this. Whether he was riding with the posse himself, or had sent Coulton, Devrin could not guess; but he knew that these men would stick with their trail until they caught up with them. Then they would shoot him down on sight, rather than give him the chance to escape again.

'They didn't take long to get together and ride out after us,' he said tightly. He glanced about him, scanning the rough terrain that lay on all sides of them. 'Maybe it would be better if we split up here. I reckon I can get them to follow me and you should be able to get back to the valley safely. They're not interested in you. So long as they can get their hands on me, I reckon they'll leave you in peace.'

'If you think that I'm going to leave you now after all the trouble I went to to save your life back there, then you're mistaken,' said the girl spiritedly. 'I know this country better than they do, maybe better than you. We can still lose them if we hurry.'

Wheeling her mount, she put it to the steep down-grade. Devrin hesitated for a fraction of a second, then followed her. Rocks and stones bounced down the slope ahead of them as their mounts went down, splay-footed, legs braced rigid on the treacherous ground. Without a saddle, Devrin was forced to twist his fingers into the horse's mane and hang on grimly as they slithered most of the way to the narrow trail that led them through tall, sky-reaching columns of red sandstone, winding away from the main trail, out in the direction of a tumbled mass of ragged boulders that seemed to have been thrust up from the ground in a crazy, haphazard fashion. At some time in the far distant past, the ground here had twisted and contracted under the influence of tremendous natural forces which had squeezed everything completely out of shape, making this a devil's playground of rocks and razor-edged chasms that opened up without warning on all sides of them so that there were long moments when it seemed to Devrin that they were riding poised on a needle edge of rock with deep crevasses all about them, threatening to engulf them with the first wrong move their mounts made.

But the girl seemed to be quite at ease here, guiding her horse as it picked its way cautiously through the fissured ground. The very nature of the terrain forced them into a slow pace, but it was soon evident to Lee that if the posse wished to catch up with them they would be forced to take this route, for the main trail wound away swiftly to the north and there was no other way down, no other route they could follow which would enable them to cut them off.

By early afternoon, they were deep inside the wilderness of rocks with deep-cut gorges that slashed through the rugged terrain. The narrow trail which they followed plunged in violent loops that hung like ladders against the sheer wall of massive stone. Further ahead, the trail tumbled into a long, spectacular earth crack, swung sharply right across a narrow plank bridge over a gorge at the bottom of which water plunged in a steep drop, the dampness of its spray reaching them even at that distance, bringing a faint chill to the air in spite of the heat of the sun. As he rode behind the girl, Devrin had the impression that this place was a vast pit, surrounded on all sides by the rising walls of rock. There seemed to be no practical crossing of the river except at this one point and thus the shoulders of the hills seemed to pinch down here, crushing down in great columns of stone.

They clattered across the swaying planks of the narrow bridge and paused on the other side. From there, it was possible to look back and see almost the whole length of the trail they had traversed during the past two hours, spread out before them in sun and shadow, winding and twisting back on itself in many places, like a snake flung down on to the hard, sun-scorched earth.

'They've started down into the canyon yonder,' said the girl, pointing. 'It will take them most of the afternoon to reach this spot. They have to travel more slowly than we did. They can't be sure that we aren't hiding in the rocks ready to ambush them.'

Devrin nodded. It was a point which had occurred to him, watching the snail-like movements of the column of men in the distance. 'Where will this trail lead us?' he asked.

'Not to the valley,' said the girl. 'That is the first place they would think of looking for you. I know a place where you'll be safe until you've had a chance to decide on your next move. Whatever you do, you have to remember that almost everyone will be against you now, especially the townsfolk. They have no real liking for Monaghan, but I think you can guess that by now, he will have seen to it that everyone believes you did this killing. Until you can prove otherwise, you'll have to stay out of sight. It's your only chance. You can't fight all of these men alone.'

'I've been wonderin' about Monaghan,' he said in a quiet, soft way.

'What about him?' asked the girl, interested. She led the way along a smooth rocky fault, up through a dense cluster of trees where the light was a pale green and there was a sharp aromatic tang of the pines in their nostrils.

'Seems to me that he must have had some other reason for wantin' to pin Bassard's murder on me than just to make sure I didn't talk about his rustlin'. After all, he must have known that I'd speak out at the trial he'd arranged for me and even if folk didn't believe it at first, it would sow the seeds of suspicion in their minds and a whole heap of things could grow from that.'

'Perhaps you just happened along and you were handy for someone to pin the blame on to.'

Devrin shook his head slowly, reflectively. 'I'd thought of that, but I'm sure there's a heap more to it than just that. From what I've heard, he and Bassard were on pretty good terms before this happened. More and more, I get to figurin' that he must have had Bassard killed on the spur of the moment.'

They rode over the rocky floor of a wide basin, turned a corner and put the bridge over the chasm behind them. The girl sat straight and tall in the saddle, her legs thrust forward in the stirrups, body swaying with the motion of the horse. It was easy to see that she had been bred to this country and he found it difficult to believe that she was the same woman he had seen stepping off the train in Fenton when he had first arrived, decked out in all of her city finery.

Her face, however bore a troubled, speculative look, lips laid closely together. Once, she turned her head and looked round at him, her glance on him, as though some hidden thought had occurred to her. They came to the summit of the trail, reached a point where they could look out over the wide range of hills and tall peaks that lifted in majestic grandeur on the northern skyline. Here she stopped and pointed a finger down the slope in front of them.

'This trail goes on over the pass and down the far side of the mountains,' she explained. 'Halfway down from the pass though, there's a small, little-known trail that leads up to the old Burro mine-workings. They won't think of searching for you there, even if they know about the shacks.'

Half an hour onward, they rode through the pass, came out on the far side where the trail widened. It was still rocky and stony underfoot, leaving no trail for their pursuers to follow.

Half a mile along the downgrade and they came upon a clearing in the straggly brush which dotted the rocks, a place which was scarcely more than a foothold at the bottom of the cliff. On either side, the grey rocks rose, tall and long-weathered, cracked in places with stunted pines marching away in a long line at the top.

'This is where we turn off,' said the girl. She smiled at the look of surprise written on his face. Edging her mount forward, she rode towards the thick tangle of green vegetation at the far side of the clearing, pushed into it and disappeared. Touching his heels to the mare's flanks, he came up to the brush, paused there for a moment, then lowered his head against an out-thrusting branch and moved into it. Whiplike branches struck at his face as he pushed through the brush but the mare was a sure-footed animal, made more wary by her experiences through the rocks below. Taking another step, they brushed through the bushes, came out on to a rocky ledge where he found

131

Mary Danaher waiting for him.

'It won't be easy along this part of the trail,' she said quietly. 'It is seldom used except by prospectors and they used burros as you can guess.'

The trail played out through rock and gravel, leading them upgrade all the time. Gravel churned under their feet whenever they were forced to dismount and lead the horses over the rougher ground. In this manner they gradually worked their way up the steep, treacherous slope, coming out occasionally on to narrow ledges along which they were forced to move slowly and with extreme caution. Breaking through tangled vine undergrowth, swinging around great masses of eroded rock, they finally made it on to a ledge that was far wider than any of the others they had traversed on their way up.

'The shacks are about half a mile along this trail,' said the girl. 'We can mount up now and go the rest of the way on horseback.'

'It sure was lucky for me that you happened along,' Devrin said, 'in more ways than one. I'd never have found this place. I've lived in this part of the territory most of my life, but I never knew this Indian trail existed.'

The girl smiled. 'I got used to riding alone when the war was on,' she said. 'I used to come up this way often in those days just to get away from everything for a while. It could be dangerous, but that only seemed to add to the thrill of everything.'

Lee nodded his head slowly. He too, could remember days when it had been good just to get away and ride a new trail, seeking the new vistas that lay around every unexpected corner. Those had been the happy, carefree days, before the dark clouds of the war had come upon the land, when there had been that tremendous feeling that they were building something new and lasting, pushing back the wide frontiers until eventually they would stretch clear to California and the wide Pacific coast. Maybe, someday, they would start again to build a better country. But the scars of war were still burned too fresh and deep in the hearts of men for them to be forgotten that easily. Peace had been declared at Appammattox Courthouse, it was true, but in spite of this, the war still went on in its own devious and subtle ways.

Presently, the trail opened out once more, became a kind of glen and the trees which had previously lined the higher reaches of the rocks moved down gently until they brushed the side of the trail. Far below, to their right, where the cliff side tumbled sheer into a precipitous drop of more than a thousand feet, they could just make out the snaking course of the main trail and off around a bend of it, picked out more by the cloud of dust kicked up by their horses than by any sign of the individual riders themselves, they could just make out the posse, crawling ant-like forward. They were still a little way from the bridge over the chasm and he could guess at the caution with which those men down there were riding. At any moment they would be expecting a fusillade of shots which could empty half the saddles in that posse. The mere fact that nothing had happened so far, would only serve to increase the tension.

He swung his attention away from them, knowing that it would be unlikely that they would find this trail. Passing between great upthrusting boulders of rock more than three stories in height, they came out into a wide clearing, flanked by tall pines and sycamores, sheltered from the sun and wind by the rocks at the rear. There were three shacks standing against the rocky wall at the back of the clearing. Two were on the verge of collapse, planks of wood lying splayed in all directions, one with its roof completely fallen in and the second with the warped boards tilted crazily. The third however, at the end of the line still appeared to be in pretty fair condition.

Riding up to it, the girl swung lightly from the saddle, led her horse forward and looped the reins around one of the wooden poles driven deep into the hard ground. Devrin dropped to the ground, stretched his legs. The long ride, clinging tightly to the animal's back had taken a lot out of him and he felt shaky in the legs as he followed the girl inside the shack.

'I've got some food in my saddlebag,' she said, pausing in the doorway. 'And we could soon start a fire. No chance of the smoke being seen up here.'

A good quarter of an hour later, they sat around the fire in the shack and ate the fried bacon and beans, washed it down with coffee made with water from the nearby creek. The night outside was very quiet and still, with the last burning vestiges of the flaming sunset gleaming down in the west between two rising pinnacles of rock that showed a dark purple against the heavens. The red-bodied pines lay thick and heavy around the clearing, muffling any sound there might have been. When he had finished, he went to the splintered doorway and leaned against it, rolling a smoke. Behind him, the girl said in a soft, low voice: 'You made up your mind what you intend to do, Lee?'

He struck the sulphur match, cupped it in his hands. Drawing the smoke down into his lungs, savouring it for a moment, he said harshly: 'I've been thinking about that all the way up here, Mary. I've got a crazy idea in my mind that explains a lot of things.'

'About Monaghan and Hague Bassard?'

'That's right.' He turned, faced her in the dimness of the twilight. 'Suppose that Monaghan was one of Quantrill's men too. Suppose he was the man who gave the orders under Quantrill. Bassard would know this and as soon as Monaghan heard I was in town, he'd get to

134

thinking that maybe Bassard would talk if I once caught up with him. So he had to plan a way of gettin' rid of Bassard and me, but he had to be clever about it. I figure that nobody else in the territory knew he rode with Quantrill. There are a lot of folk in the town and in the small ranches around Fenton who were hurt by Quantrill and his raiders. I'm not the only one. If they discovered that Monaghan gave the orders and led some of those rebels against the settlements, they'd wreak their own vengeance on him.'

'So he killed Bassard and framed you for the murder.'

'Exactly. And it would be Monaghan who tried to kill your father when he was bringin' me news of Bassard.' Devrin's smile was a tight streak against his features and the faint red sheen of the flickering firelight from inside the cabin threw its bronzed highlights over his face, emphasising the prominent cheekbones, making it look hard and rugged. The girl's eyes narrowed on him for a moment and then widened in sudden appraisal. He saw the change on her lips, watched the small gust of expression go over her face.

'How can you ever hope to prove it, even if it is true?' she asked.

'There are always ways of gettin' at a man,' he said quietly, his tone firm and even. 'Could be that in a couple of days he'll figure that I've ridden out of the territory. When he doesn't find me at your place, or in town, he'll guess I've gone.'

'You won't get the sheriff to back you, even if you do get proof. It's my belief that Monaghan has some powerful hold over him.'

'There must be several men in town who would believe it, powerful men,' he muttered. He drew deeply on the cigarette, stared down at the growing tip in the dimness. 'Do you think that you could talk with these men? Your

135

father would know who they are and who can be trusted. The smaller ranchers are having their cattle rustled by Monaghan's men. That much I know for a fact. They may decide to throw in their lot against Monaghan when the times comes.'

The girl looked dubious for a moment, then nodded. 'It's the only chance there is,' she admitted gravely, apparently turning the possibilities over in her mind. She watched him as she said it and when she saw his reassuring smile, her expression lightened visibly and she smiled back at him. She waited for some kind of answer from him, but when none was forthcoming, she moved out into the clearing, stood staring out to the east where the round yellow face of the moon was beginning to show faintly through the branches of the pines.

'I'll ride down into the town at sun-up,' she said quietly. 'What will you do?'

'I'll stay here for a couple of days,' he murmured easily. 'Then I'll ride down and complete my unfinished business with Monaghan. This time though, I shall be ridin' in there with my eyes open.'

When he had finished breakfast the next morning, Devrin moved out at once into the bright sunlight which flooded down the mountain side, breathing in the thin, winey air. The girl came out a few moments later and waited while he saddled her horse for her, then swung up into the saddle, looked down at him for a long moment with concern on her face. Very softly, she said: 'Whatever you do, promise me you won't take any foolish risks, Lee,'

He smiled up at her. 'I promise,' he said gently. 'You're sure you know the way down?'

'I could find it in the dark,' she said reassuringly. She drew in a deep breath, then let it fall. Her smile pinched out a little. 'Whatever happens down there, don't underestimate Monaghan. He's clever and he'll watch every angle.'

'I'll be careful.' He stood back as she touched spurs to her mount. A moment later, she turned a bend in the trail and vanished from sight. He stood quite still, listening to the echoes, then turned and went back into the cabin. For a moment, the need to mount up and have it out with Monaghan as soon as possible was so strong within him that he found it almost impossible to fight down and he looked out over the looping ridges of the hills as if he could see far off into the blue-hazed distance, off as far as the Double C ranch. Then, with an effort, he relaxed.

Squatting against the side of the shack, he stared off into the distance, grateful for the rest and the chance to do a little straight thinking. So far he had been on the run with Monaghan calling the tune, making him jump through the hoop and giving him no chance to get things sorted out properly in his mind. He knew instinctively that he had little chance of bucking the full force of men that Monaghan could swing against him. All he wished was an even chance at the other, an even encounter, when he felt certain he could force the other into admitting his own implication in the murder of Hague Bassard and equally important, in the slaughter of those innocent men and women during Quantrill's raids on this part of the territory.

He eased his body into a more comfortable position as the sunlight waxed stronger in the clearing, sparkling through the swaying branches, and the heat began to grow, making itself felt. Bitterness welled up inside him as he thought of what must have happened here when Quantrill's killers swept down on the small farms and ranches, burning, killing and looting. The savage hatred of the world and the men in it, surged up within his mind, even stronger than before. Would it ever ease up on him? he wondered wearily, or would it keep digging its sharply-rowelled spurs into him just when he thought he had forgotten it for good?

He felt the fierce desire to fight these men in their own way, matching cruelty and ruthlessness with a savagery all his own. It was the only thing they understood, the only way in which they knew how to fight. If the world itself made cruelty its byword, then he would live himself by those rules, would ask for no quarter and give none in return. He would hunt Monaghan and all others like him to the trail's end, make them beg for mercy, watch all of their pride and manhood ooze out of them until they were mere empty shells of what they had once been. Only then would he be completely satisfied and only then would he feel whole and at ease again.

He straightened up, brought his tightly-clenched fists together and stared down at his interlocked fingers. He felt ridden by the intensity of his feeling and knew that he would have to keep it tightly under control, would have to be completely and utterly dispassionate when it came to facing down Monaghan.

With a conscious mental effort, he brought his mind back to the present. His own position was precarious. He believed Mary Danaher when she had said that it was highly unlikely that they would find him up here, but he still had to ride down and find Monaghan and that would be far from easy. But at the moment he was clear of the other. Just as he had been hunted, now he was in a position to hunt in return.

The chances were even, fifty-fifty. Maybe, he thought with a fierce sense of jubilation. Monaghan didn't know that yet. By now, the posse would have given up their search of these hills. They would probably have ridden out to Danaher's ranch, searched there for him, and not finding him, would have gone back to town with word of his disappearance for Monaghan. For a moment he wondered whether they would take any further action against Clem Danaher once they discovered that he was still alive, but somehow he doubted this. He had brought it out into the open at his trial, and he judged that Monaghan would not want to take the risk of trying anything more. He had succeeded in his purpose of implicating him with Bassard's death and there was nothing that Clem could do to change that.

# GUN RECKONING

The ledge was long and wide, perhaps half a mile in length and it lifted some fifty feet above the rest of the flat desert. In the bright silver moonlight, Lee Devrin sat on a small mound and stared intently about him. He had slept well for the two days he had spent at the shack and he no longer felt the need for sleep. His body was well rested, the bruises healed and his eyes took in everything, his face tensed and inscrutable.

The sand around him would muffle the sound of horses even in the deep, intense stillness that had dropped all about him at the going down of the sun three hours earlier. The moon had risen an hour after full darkness and now gave sufficient light to see by, although it threw deep slashes of midnight shadow over the rising dunes and gullies that stretched out to the far horizons. He shivered a little in the cold night air and pulled the collar of the mackinaw jacket around his neck. Out here, in the deep, pendant stillness of the desert night a man's imagination could run to all kinds of ideas, he reflected.

Thrusting his legs out in front of him, he rolled himself a smoke, ducking his head low as he lit it, keeping himself well into the moonthrown shadow of the mound, deliberately easing his body against the hard rocks. Even the

140

faint, intermittent red glow from a burning cigarette could be seen half a mile away by a keen-eyed marksman and many a man had died because he had neglected this elementary precaution.

He smoked the cigarette slowly, feeling it bring some of the warmth and feeling back into his body. It would become even colder as the night went on, but he still felt no need to sleep. He was sated with it now. Most of the time he had spent in the shack had been absorbed into thinking things out, trying to form some kind of workable plan in his mind. But too much was going to depend on Monaghan's actions for him to be able to plan ahead to any great extent.

It was almost one o'clock in the morning when he finally stirred himself as the faint drumming of hooves sounded in the distance. It was impossible to tell how many there were or how far away the riders were but of one thing he felt sure. They could be only Monaghan's men, or the posse, still scouring the territory for him. He smiled grimly in the white moonlight. That could only mean that Monaghan was still afraid, still not certain that he had pulled out.

The stretch of desert that ran away from the bottom of the ledge was flat, smooth, as far as the eye could see with only a single column of sandstone far off to his left, like a vast finger of stone pointing accusingly at the moon. He moved forward swiftly to the rim of the ledge and knelt close to his horse, ready to place a hand over the mare's mouth if those other horses came close enough for her to scent them.

At first, he could make out nothing in the eerie moon-glow, as he searched with eyes and ears, every nerve and fibre of his being pulled taut as piano wire through his body, his flesh quivering with apprehension. Then, off to the right, approaching the sandstone column, he saw the

141

tightly-knit bunch of riders, clustered close together and spurring their mounts at a swift pace across the desert. He reckoned that they were best part of two miles away, but edging slightly in his direction. If they continued on their present course, they would pass within half a mile of his hiding place, he guessed.

Holding his breath until it hurt in his lungs, he edged back a little way from the rocky rim. The riders swung closer, the muffled sound of the hoofbeats moving ahead of them. Devrin reckoned that there were a dozen or fifteen of them, about as many as he had earlier figured there had been in the posse. A moment later, his horse moved slightly on the rocks, its shoes striking a hard sound that seemed explosively loud in the stillness.

Devrin murmured softly to the animal and it stood quite still, a little unsure of itself. Had those men heard the faint sound? he wondered tensely. They would be watching and listening for anything that would give them a clue to his whereabouts. But they continued on their undeviating course and as they swept by, he saw the man leading them, felt certain that he had recognised the black-bearded man he had caught rustling that stock some days before. So these were Double C riders. He felt a little shiver pass through him as riders and sound faded into the distance. The cold night air struck through his clothing, chilling him to the bone.

'They've gone,' he said softly, speaking to the horse. 'But I figure we ain't safe yet, by a long way. They may ride on for a little while and then decide to backtrack.'

There would be no sleep for him during the rest of the night even if he had felt the need for rest. He moved around on the ledge until he found a small hollow, screened from the wind by a ring of cactus. The dry, stiff plants rustled eerily and continuously in the wind, sounding like a soul in torment, but it would serve to keep him wide awake and it was, at least, the best defensive position he could see.

He remained there for an hour until sure that the bunch of riders were not heading back, then decided to move on. The further he travelled by night, the less were the chances of being seen by Monaghan's men. It was quite a simple matter for him to take his directions from the moon and stars and with the cool, clear air blowing about him, he made good progress. Anger and the burning desire for vengeance was the force which drove him on during the long hours.

By dawn, he had covered ten miles, knew that he was somewhere on the northern edge of the Double C range. He rested up for a little while in a clump of mesquite and soapweed, the only plants which managed to survive in this stretch of the desert. The sun came up half an hour later and the warmth, when it came, was a welcome relief from the terrible, bitter cold of the night but within an hour, it was soaking into his body until he felt sickened by the sunglare, the perspiration boiling out of him from every pore, eyes and flesh burned by the inferno breeze that stirred little eddies of sand from the crests of the dunes, flinging its irritating grains into his face. The crushing sunblast pressed down on him like the flat of a mighty hand, and every breath brought the choking rawness to his throat and lungs.

For several hours, he was forced to endure a purgatory on earth. He had no water left and the few waterholes that he did come across were all bone dry, the earth cracked by the blistering heat.

The most pressing of his worries now was to find water. By this time, he figured he had ridden far enough to be safe enough from prying eyes. He guessed that the last place Monaghan would think of looking for him would be on his own land. But unless he could find water somewhere and soon he might become so weak than he would be unable to ride any further. Having no saddle, made riding more difficult. A feeling of helplessness rose within him and stayed with him as the sun rose higher in the sky and the shadows on either side of him shortened until they were almost non-existent. At length, he reached a stretch of rough country, sparsely covered by tufts of grass that lifted clear of the desert, climbing steeply into an area of tumbled boulders and tall, spired rocks, etched and eroded into fantastic shapes by long geological ages of sun and wind.

Behind a massive spire of rock, thick at the base, tapering into a tall, slender column that rose for almost two hundred feet into the air lay a mass of crags and rocks, a maze of immense bosses of stone that were piled high in a titanic confusion. He paused on the rim of this great natural amphitheatre, uncertain. There would be no water in there, he told himself wearily but it might take him the rest of the day and part of the night as well to work his way around it and he could not afford to waste all that precious time. If he was forced to deviate from the trail he was following too much, the chances were that he could lose his way and wander in circles until he died of thirst. He reached a sudden decision, put the horse forward into the maze. There seemed to be a narrow trail of sorts, but it petered out on several occasions, never running straight and true through the great formations of stone. He was well into the rocks when he picked out the faint sound close by. Reining up, he listened intently, scarcely able to believe his ears. The sound of running water reached him from a little way off the trail to his right and he tugged sharply on the mare's mane, bringing its head round. Two minutes later, they located the small waterfall that splashed down into a shallow pool at the base of the rocks, the water sparkling brilliantly in the flooding sunlight. He let the horse drink a little while he cupped his hands under the waterfall, drinking in quick gulps, then placing his hat underneath, filling it to the brim and pouring it over his head.

Filling the empty canteen, he corked it securely, looping the leather strap into his belt. The mare lifted her head, protesting as he pulled her away from the water. She had not drunk as much as she would have liked, but he knew that they still had the worst part of the day to come yet and it was better to ride dry than sweat out a lot of water.

Refreshed, he continued on through the rocks, still moving south towards the Double C range, reaching it just as the sun was weltering towards the far hills, purpling the heavens. The journey now was far more pleasant. Not only was the heat diminishing, but the ground underfoot consisted of soft brown soil and lush green grass. Even the mare seemed to have forgotten her weariness and they made good progress, moving at a steady lope in the direction of the ranch house, Devrin sitting tall as he kept a close, keen watch for any sign of trouble.

He spotted a herd on one of the hills in the distance just before it became too dark to make out any details, but the shifting black mass was too far away for there to be any chance of him having been seen by any of the hired hands and he cut left, swinging off the trail, topping a low rise half an hour later and coming in sight of the ranch buildings. Lights were showing in two of the windows and he remained there for several minutes, watching the place. In all of that time, there was no movement outside the buildings and he also noticed that there were no horses in the circular corral at the edge of the courtyard. That, he figured, could mean only one thing. Most of the men had ridden out, were probably still scouring the countryside for him, leaving the rest to watch the herd.

He rode part of the way down the lee of the hill, then swung down and went the rest of the way on foot, the gun in his hand, finger ready on the trigger. Still no movement as he got to the edge of the courtyard. He stood quite still for a long moment, listening. When he heard nothing, he circled around, cut across the dust, came up to the wall at the side of the ranch house and placed his ear against it. Again, he heard nothing from inside, no sound of any voices. Moving slowly to the corner of the building, he was on the point of moving out and edging towards the door when it opened suddenly, a shaft of lamplight spilled out into the courtyard and a dimly seen figure stepped out on to the porch.

The other was smoking a cigarette and peering into the dimness, Devrin noticed that it was the man who had kept watch over him when he had been shackled inside the barn. Very slowly, he moved away from the wall of the building, He saw the other start as he caught the movement at the edge of his vision, saw the man's hand drop towards the gun at his waist. Then he froze as Devrin's voice came to him out of the night.

'Touch that gunbutt and there'll be a bullet in you.'

The other hesitated, then said quaveringly. 'That you, Devrin?'

'The same,' said Lee. He walked forward carefully until he came up to the other. 'How many are inside?'

'Nobody,' said the man in a harsh whisper. 'I'm alone here. The others are out lookin' for you.'

'All right, turn around,' he ordered. The other obeyed at once. Reaching out, Devrin pulled the other's gun from its holster and tossed it across the courtyard where it fell against one of the corral posts. 'Now step away from the building. Over to the side yonder.'

Holding his hands over his head, the other did as he was ordered. 'You'd better tell me the truth.' Devrin's voice was crisp, deadly. 'I want to know where Monaghan is right now and who's with him.'

'He rode into town late this afternoon,' said the other quickly, the words spilling over themselves in his hurry to get them out. 'There are only Jason and Riller with him. The others are with Clem and Mander, lookin' for you.'

'Why'd he go into town?'

'I don't know. He doesn't tell me anythin'. That's the truth, Devrin. Honest to God it is.'

'What do you know about God?' Devrin said harshly. 'Your orders before were to let me get away but not to let it look too easy. That's true, isn't it?'

When the other did not reply, he ground the barrel of the Colt into the other's back, the foresight cutting in through the man's shirt. He moaned a little with the pain, tried to move away from the gun. 'Yes, damn you,' he snarled suddenly, 'Monaghan wanted you to get away so that he could pin the killin' of Hague Bassard on to you.'

'That's how I figured it,' Devrin said tightly. 'You know why he wanted Bassard dead?'

'No. I swear I don't. Maybe they quarrelled. Maybe Bassard wanted more than the foreman's job here. There was some trouble when they first started up this place. Bassard wanted to ride west, start afresh out in California, but it seemed that Monaghan knew somethin' about his past, and he never made it. He had to stay here and work for Monaghan whether he liked it or not.'

'So that was it.' Devrin nodded to himself in the darkness. He said tersely. 'Get your horse. You're ridin' with me into town. There are some folk there who will be plenty interested in hearin' this.'

'You goin' to turn me in to the sheriff?' As the other spoke, Devrin heard the faint note of relief in the man's voice.

'No. I'm turning you over to Clem Danaher and some

of the ranchers. I've learned a lot in the past few days. Enough to know that Coulton and Monaghan are in cahoots and that I'd be stupid to turn you over to Coulton. You'd walk out of jail within minutes.'

He kept the gun trained on the other as he brought his horse out from the stables. On the way out, Devrin picked out a saddle for himself, slapped it on to the mare, tightened the cinch, not once taking his eyes off the other.

'Now mount up and don't try any tricks. After what has happened, I'll feel plenty justified in shootin' you.'

The other's brows came down, scowling, but he did as he was told. Together they rode out of the courtyard, taking the trail that led into Fenton.

The moon was still balanced low on the horizon when they came within sight of the town, sprawling in a mass of shadow on either side of the main street. Devrin pulled his mount to a walk, signalled to the other to do likewise. As far as he knew, the only man in town who could really be trusted was Doc Stratton. He had been his father's friend and now, although he was old and had ceased to practice, Devrin knew he would still help in the fight against Monaghan.

'Where do you figure on goin' now?' asked the other, grinning a little. 'By now, Monaghan will have the place swarming with men. Coulton's men. They had orders to stay in town and keep their eyes open just in case you did try to come back. That's why the rest of the boys from the ranch were out lookin' for you.'

'I'd already figured on that,' Lee told him quietly. He saw the other's triumphant expression change. He drifted forward with caution. There were several horses hitched to the rails in front of the two saloons near the middle of the town and judging from the sounds of revelry which reached them faintly, the men were enjoying themselves, obviously not taking their task of watching for him too seriously.

Turning off the main street, he motioned the other down one of the narrow side streets, stopping in front of the lowroofed building. There was a single light showing in one of the windows. Turning to the other, he said sharply: 'All right. This is as far as you go. Get down.'

The other hesitated, then saw Devrin's hand move suggestively towards the gun at his waist, decided that discretion was the better part of valour now and got down from the saddle. Going forward, Devrin knocked softly on the door. A few moments later, he heard the faint sound of footsteps and then the metallic rattle of a chair. The door opened a few inches.

'Yes. Who is it?'

'Me, Lee Devrin, Doc. I need your help.'

'Lee. Come inside, my boy.' The other opened the door, glanced up at him and then at the man standing close by. 'And who's this?'

'This is one of Monaghan's men. I want you to be a witness to what he has to say and then keep him here. Think you can do that?'

There was a hard look on the old doctor's face as he motioned the two men inside. He said tightly, 'From what I now know of Monaghan, I guess this *hombre* is a hard case like the other killers who are ridin' with him?'

'That's right,' Devrin nodded. 'I don't like askin' you to do this, but there's nobody else in town I can really trust. The sheriff is in cahoots with Monaghan and right now they're scourin' the town for me. Monaghan's killers are lookin' for me outside the town.'

'I know.' The other nodded his head wisely.

'You know?' said Devrin, surprised. 'But how?'

'Mary Danaher and her father were here less than an hour ago. They're in town now to talk with some of the smaller ranchers. She explained to me what had happened, said that you might be along, but I expected you to come alone.'

'I met this *hombre* at the Double C ranch. He was the one who kept watch while they held me prisoner there the day that Hague Bassard was killed. His testimony clears me.'

Doc Stratton turned his gaze on the sullen-faced man, then gave a wise nod. 'I can recognise the type,' he said softly. Going into one of the rooms, he came back a few moments later with a long-barrelled revolver. The weapon seemed ancient, but Devrin did not doubt that it was loaded and also that the other would not hesitate to use it if he had to. 'I'll make sure he doesn't get away, Lee,' he said firmly. 'What do you intend to do now?'

'I've got some unfinished business with Monaghan,' Devrin said grimly. 'I guess he'll be around town some-place.'

'Be careful. Coulton has men posted everywhere just in case you show up. Most of these men are honest citizens, but they believe that you killed Bassard and they won't hesitate to shoot to kill if they see you.' Stratton glanced at the man over by the wall. 'Why don't we get this *hombre* to talk to them? Once they know what really happened, these men will be on your side. They don't like Monaghan any more than you do. But—'

'We don't have time for that,' Lee said quietly. 'Like you say, Coulton has men everywhere. This fella has only to yell out that we've caught him and they'll shoot us down before we have any chance to explain.'

'That may be so as far as you're concerned,' agreed the other. 'But there are still a lot of folk in town who know and trust me. I can get them to listen.'

Devrin's eyes hardened. 'The chances are you'd never succeed. Better stay here until I've found Monaghan and see to it that this *hombre* doesn't get away. He'll shoot you in the back like those other coyotes would if he gets half a chance.'

'I'll watch him, never you fear,' affirmed the other. Devrin hesitated in spite of the other's assurance. But there was no other choice open to him. He did not like leaving Stratton with this killer, but it had to be done. Inwardly, he hoped that Mary Danaher and her father had some success with the ranchers. At the moment, it seemed their only chance.

When he reached the shadows at the end of the alley, he paused there for a whole minute to have a good look around him. He tried to identify some of the horses tethered outside the saloons, but at that distance it was impossible to do so. The tinkling of a tinny piano reached him from across the street and as he watched, the swing doors of the nearer saloon opened and a drunk staggered out on to the boardwalk, paused teetering on the edge before falling on to his knees in the dusty street. He knelt there for a long moment, still clutching a bottle in his hands. Then he raised it to his lips, let the liquor trickle down his throat, spilling some of it down the front of his shirt. He remained like that, swaying a tittle, until the bottle was empty, then hurled it away from him, somehow managed to get to his feet and staggered with a swaying, lurching motion along the street in Lee's direction.

He waited until the other had drawn level with the alley, then stepped out, saw the other sway backward, eyes widening a little at his sudden appearance. Grasping the drunk by the front of his shirt, Devrin pulled him back into the alley, thrust him against the wall, holding the man there as he almost fell forward, collapsing on to his knees again.

'What d'you want?' muttered the other thickly. 'This a

hold-up? If it is, you're plumb out of luck. I spent my last coin in the saloon.'

'I don't want your money,' Devrin said thickly. He tightened his grip on the other. 'I want to know whether Monaghan is in the saloon.'

'Monaghan?' murmured the drunk. He peered up at Devrin out of bloodshot eyes, lips hanging slackly open. The smell of whiskey almost knocked Devrin down. 'Sure he's there. Been there most of the night with a bunch of his men. You lookin' for him?'

'That's right,' Devrin nodded, released his hold on the other. The man swayed against him heavily for a moment, clung to him to regain his balance, then pulled himself upright with an effort, turned and staggered off along the alley, vanishing into the darkness at the far end. Devrin sucked in a sharp gust of air. Now, at least, he knew where he stood. Hitching the gunbelt a little higher around his waist, he moved out on to the boardwalk, followed the front of the stores on that side of the street until he was opposite the saloon, glanced up and down the street for a few seconds, saw no one, then stepped firmly across to the other side. He paused for only a few moments, then made his way around to the side of the building. There was a balcony around the wall here just below the second storey. He jumped for it, felt his fingers catch at the bottom and hung there, all of his weight dragging down on his arm and shoulder muscles. With a tremendous heave, he succeeded in pulling himself up, hooking his elbows over the rail, his chest crashing painfully against the hard metal.

He paused there for a moment, dragging air down into his tortured lungs, then pulled himself over, landing lightly on his feet on the balcony. The window in front of him was half-open and lifting it cautiously, he slipped into the darkened room that lay beyond. Standing quite still,

he waited until his eyes had grown accustomed to the
gloom before moving gingerly forward, placing one foot
carefully in front of the other. He let his weight fall slow
and easy, edged forward until his outstretched fingers
rapped softly against the wooden door on the side of the
room. Small as the sound was, it seemed to echo and
reverberate through the whole building, magnified many
times by his mind. He stopped dead in his tracks, heard
nothing to indicate that the sound had been noticed, but
in spite of this, an unaccustomed coolness ruffled the
small hairs on the back of his neck. Twisting the handle
slowly, he opened the door and stepped through, found
himself in a short passage. Here he guessed there would
be a stairway leading down into the saloon below. These
were evidently the living quarters of the owner and his
family. He looked to right and left, discovered nothing,
but moved slowly forward until his outstretched foot
encountered nothing. Going down on to his haunches,
he explored the place with his fingers, discovered the
stairs that led down, guessed that there was a closed door
at the bottom. Cautiously, making no sound, he moved
down them, saw as he drew nearer to the bottom that
there was a faint crack of light showing just beneath the
door.

Sucking in a long, heavy gust of wind, he let it come out
again in slow pinches, checked the guns, then slipped
them back into their holsters. Through the thickness of
the door he could hear the musical chords of the piano
and the raucous yelling of the men in the bar.

Turning the handle, he found the door unlocked and
opened it gently. There was a further flight of stairs on the
other side, twisting away at right angles to those he had
just descended which explained why the light shining
beneath the door had been so faint. At the bottom of the
stairs, he noticed the wooden railing, knew that they

would lead him out at the top of the flight of stairs which led down into the saloon.

He stood rigid for a long moment, then told himself that nothing would be gained by hesitation, that he had the one big advantage of surprise. As yet, Monaghan did not have an inkling of his presence there.

Moving to the end of the stairs, he found himself looking down on to the heads of the men below him. He stood quite still, searching around until he spotted Monaghan. The rancher was seated at one of the tables in the corner of the room. There were three men with him, one the short wiry man who had been branding the rustled cattle when Devrin had first ridden on to the Double C range. The other two he did not recognise but guessed they were also some of Monaghan's men. Warily, he let his gaze flick over the other men in the saloon. Most of them would be storekeepers and cardsharps, who would keep out of any gunplay if it came to a showdown. Licking his lips, he drew the Colts from their holsters and stepped out on to the wide stairway. He was halfway down before anyone noticed him.

Devrin knew that he had at least four men to deal with in the saloon, but that the chances were there could be more than five times that number if he hesitated too long. Within minutes, the place could be swarming with Coulton and his men,

'Don't move, any of you!' Devrin's voice, cold and incisive, cut like the lash of a whip across the low, muted murmur of conversation. The man with the bowler hat seated at the piano pushed his stool back a couple of feet, sat quite still with a frightened look on his face, eyes wide, mouth hanging slackly open.

Through narrowed eyes, Devrin saw one of the men with Monaghan shift his right hand very slightly. 'Don't try to be brave,' he said harshly. 'That goes for all of you here.

I've got business only with Monaghan there, the man who killed Hague Bassard. Now everybody let their guns drop or they'll be holding a bullet by the time I count three and it won't be in any gun!'

Reluctantly, the three men with Monaghan pulled their guns and let them fall clattering to the floor at their feet. The other men at the tables and ranged along the bar did likewise. Only Monaghan himself made no move and there was a thin, cold smile fixed on his face.

'If you're expectin' me to obey that order, Devrin, then you're mistaken,' he said curtly. 'I don't take orders from cold-blooded murderers. You killed Hague and you can't prove otherwise.'

'That's where you're wrong, Monaghan. You see, I've got the man who kept me prisoner in your barn the day that Bassard was killed. And he's talked. By now, most of the town will know the truth. I wouldn't give much for your chances now.'

'You're lyin'!' snapped the other, speaking thickly through his teeth. There was a look of trapped fear on his face now which he could not hide and it was evident he knew that Devrin was speaking the truth.

'Bassard was killed because he was the only man around here who knew that you were one of Quantrill's trusted lieutenants, that you were the man who gave the orders when they swept down and slaughtered the folk in this area, burned their ranches to the ground. Bassard was weak-willed, wanted to get out, but you held him here with the threat of exposing him if he went against you. When I rode in and started nosin' around you soon guessed that once I got to Bassard, he'd talk his head off, tellin' me everythin' and that was somethin' you didn't want. So you arranged it that Bassard died. You shot him in the back while I was kept hog-tied in that barn of yours. But you'd given orders that I was to be allowed to get away so that the blame for Bassard's murder could be pinned on me. That way, you'd be rid of both of us.'

'You're a dirty liar, Devrin!' snapped the other viciously. His voice was choked with rage. 'You think you can get away with somethin' like this. That hand of mine will say anythin' when he has a gun stuck in his back. Anybody would. When we have you safely under lock and key, he'll tell the truth then and—'

The expression on the other's pallid features changed abruptly. His talk had been nothing but a feint to take Devrin's attention off what he really intended to do. With a sudden heave, he thrust the table over, dropped down behind it, pulling a gun as he did so. The shot hummed within an inch of Devrin's head, thudding into the railing, biting a piece of wood out of it. Dropping on to one knee, Lee sent a couple of shots, one on either side of the table. One of the other men, reaching for his gun, snatched his hand back quickly as a slug ploughed into the floor close to his fingers.

Monaghan slammed another couple of shots at where Devrin crouched, then scuttled out from behind the table, diving for the bar. Swiftly, instinctively, Devrin swung the Colt in his hand, squeezed off a single shot, felt the heavy weapon buck against his wrist. Down below, Monaghan seemed to pause in mid-air, his body almost horizontal. He remained flat on his stomach, his fingers still gripping the smoking gun, but relaxing slowly, releasing their grip as his whole body relaxed. Flopping on to his face, a long, rattling sigh came out of him, then he lay still.

Slowly, his gun covering the three men at the corner table, Devrin moved down the stairs, went over to Monaghan's body and turned it over with his boot. The limpness told him everything he wanted to know. Monaghan had pulled his last trick.

Thrusting the gun back into his holster, he turned to

look at the three men. 'If any of you want to try for your guns, it's all right by me,' he said thinly. None of them made any move. The death of Monaghan seemed to have stunned them all.

Then a sharp voice from the doorway said: 'All right. Lift your hands, Devrin! Keep 'em well away from those guns.'

Sheriff Coulton stepped into the saloon. His gaze took in Monaghan's body lying near the bar. 'Guess this time we'll really hang you,' he said coldly.

He advanced into the room, a faint grin on his face. 'Could be that I'd be within my rights as a lawman to shoot you down here and now.'

'You won't be shooting anybody.' Coulton stiffened abruptly. Clem Danaher pushed his way into the saloon, limping a little, but the rifle in his hands was as steady as a rock as he held it levelled on the sheriff. 'We've got all the evidence we need to tie you in with Monaghan and his rustlin'. Now drop that gun or I'll break your spine with a rifle bullet.'

Coulton let the gun fall to the floor. There was a tight look of defeat on his face as Danaher came forward, picked up the gun and thrust it into his belt. 'I reckon that just about winds this deal up,' he said calmly. 'With Monaghan dead, that smashes the Double C. Those men of his still out there in the desert will fade over the hill when they hear of this. He was the only one who held them here. As for you, Coulton, I guess the Citizens' Committee will soon decide on the suitable punishment for a crooked lawman.'

While a couple of the men hustled Coulton away, Danaher glanced at Lee. 'You all right?' he asked. 'When Stratton told us what had happened, I guessed you'd come here tryin' to do this all by yourself.'

'Seemed to me the only thing to do in the circumstances,' Lee said. He felt suddenly weary, empty inside.

The other nodded. 'I'm goin' to have a drink,' he said quietly. A pause, then: 'Mary is waitin' outside, son. Guess I can drink alone for once.'